Globetrotter

Globetrotter

DAVID ALBAHARI

TRANSLATED BY ELLEN ELIAS-BURSAĆ

YALE UNIVERSITY PRESS ■ NEW HAVEN & LONDON

A MARGELLOS
WORLD REPUBLIC OF LETTERS BOOK

The Margellos World Republic of Letters is dedicated to making literary works from around the globe available in English through translation. It brings to the English-speaking world the work of leading poets, novelists, essayists, philosophers, and playwrights from Europe, Latin America, Africa, Asia, and the Middle East to stimulate international discourse and creative exchange.

English translation © 2014 by Yale University. Translated by Ellen Elias-Bursać. Originally published as *Svetski Putnik* by Stubovi kulture, Belgrade, 2001. Copyright © 2001 by David Albahari.

The translator acknowledges the assistance of the Banff International Literary Translation Centre at the Art Centre in Banff, Alberta, Canada.

Yale University Press books may be purchased in quantity for educational, business, or promotional use. For information, please e-mail sales.press@yale.edu (U.S. office) or sales@yaleup.co.uk (U.K. office).

Set in Electra and Nobel type by Tseng Information Systems Inc., Durham, NC. Printed in the United States of America.

Library of Congress Cataloging-in-Publication Data
Albahari, David, 1948–
[Svetski putnik. English]
Globetrotter / David Albahari ; translated by Ellen Elias-Bursać.
pages cm. — (The Margellos World Republic of Letters)
ISBN 978-0-300-20132-1 (paperback)
I. Elias-Bursać, Ellen. II. Title.
PG1419.1.L335S9413 2014
891.8'2354—dc23

2014005689

A catalogue record for this book is available from the British Library.

This paper meets the requirements of ANSI/NISO Z39.48–1992 (Permanence of Paper).

10 9 8 7 6 5 4 3 2 1

CONTENTS

GLOBETROTTER

Everything in this book is imaginary, only Banff is real.

C ities are like women, I said to Daniel Atijas when we met at the Centre in Banff on June 11, 1998. You like the way some look, I said, and others you like for what they are on the inside. Some cities are neither, I said, and you are indifferent when you find yourself there, just as you are indifferent, I said, by the side of certain women. They are colorless, I said, like air. I thought he'd say air is not colorless—he struck me as that type of person, the kind who always, without being overbearing, states things as they are—but he only sipped his soup and glanced out the window from time to time. Banff, I continued, is something else again, though this is not obvious at first, especially if you spend only a day or two here the way most people do, but if you stick around longer, I said, for a week, say, you will see what has intrigued me here for years: the special knack Banff has of appearing in two forms at once, as two extremes, one of which, if I dare pursue my parallel with women, I said, expresses the eternal virgin; the other, the lusty strumpet. Here I stopped. I had expected him to blink when he heard that last word—he struck me as the type who would be ready to blink, who'd feel no compulsion to hide honest embarrassment—but he merely set down his spoon and reached for the salad. Someone else might have been discouraged by having their expectations trounced twice, especially those who dread unpredictability, in which group I do not, I am glad to say, count myself, so in Daniel Atijas's refusal to be candid—sure as I was of my appraisal—I could recognize and relish this degree of unpredictability, for it is exactly what challenges us and attracts us to a person. I rubbed my hands together under the table and said: This is why every time I come to Banff I start by thinking I'll write a book about it, though I know I never will; I am a painter, not a writer, and if I were a master of words, I would discard my paintbrush and paints straightaway because being a writer is so much better for the health than being a painter, because despite all the warnings about the dangers of computer and monitor radiation, at least a writer needn't inhale toxic fumes, poison himself with his work—and here I stopped, not knowing how to get myself back to the writing of a book about Banff. But Daniel Atijas, as if he had been waiting, set down his knife and fork, coughed, and said: I have never been this high up in mountains; I am a child of the plains. I could have fallen straight off my chair, I was so surprised, not because he had finally spoken—after all, I had been chatting away precisely to draw him out—but because this hadn't even occurred to me, and it should have, for I, too, am a child of the plains, born in Saskatchewan, where, by the way, I live, so I should have recognized in him the reflection of his plains, which, I later learned, are called Vojvodina, for that makes us more similar than either of us might have reckoned. I did not, however, fall off my chair, though just in case, I firmly gripped the table edge, but then Daniel Atijas stood up, said he had to leave, and left. There are people who, when they go, take something with them. Hard to say just what. Something opens in a person, and then something is gone: I don't know if I can say it any better. Daniel Atijas left and I sat there, choking on emotions in which I had ceased believing long ago. I repeated to myself several times, Steady now, then I took a deep breath and dropped my hands into my lap. After all, Daniel Atijas had struck me as the type who ups and goes like that, just as he had the evening before, when, excusing himself and blaming jet lag, he left the reception, held in his honor, after giving his talk and responding to questions for twenty minutes. I had sat in the second row during the talk, right behind the president of the Banff Centre and his wife. The president's shoulder was specked with flakes of dandruff. Daniel Atijas waved his arms frequently as he talked, as if short of words, though he spoke readily in English. His pronunciation was hard-edged, Slavic, but still easily understood. He did not hide his feelings, and his voice quavered quite audibly several times, cracking before he reached the last lines. The president's wife took out her handkerchief each time and dabbed the corners of her eyes as if to console them. Continuing to gesticulate, Daniel Atijas spoke of the relationship between history and literature in his country, in his former country, he said, or rather in the five countries that came out of the one that no longer existed. His voice quavered. Several days later, when I reminded him of this, I added that I, too, had trembled while listening to reports about the referendum on the secession of Quebec. We each have our own hell, replied Daniel Atijas. Had I known, at the talk, he would say this, I would have better understood his behavior; I would have known that his hell was public speaking. Despite his emotions, quavering voice, and pointed humor, Daniel Atijas was forever digging in with his defenses. Instead of getting closer to his listeners, he pulled away, so at one point I felt like standing up and drawing him to me, to all of us. He looked, after all, like someone who is always inward bound, regardless of where he is headed. I told him so once: we were on the path running down by the city cemetery, and I stopped a little theatrically and, spreading my arms, said he struck me as someone who, no matter where he went, was always inward bound, to which he replied with a chuckle that it made no difference, since all of us end up in the same place. No doubt, I said, but not at the same cemetery. I have spent my whole life, I said, in Saskatchewan, in Saskatoon, and I won't be changing towns in death. Daniel Atijas laughed again. At the talk, however, he was serious, even when he interjected humor, always at an apt juncture, to ease the tension of his impassioned narrative. I didn't for a moment take my eyes off his face at the talk or on the path by the cemetery. After the talk I was barely able to hold my focus on the words the president's wife was saying, and suddenly I wanted, right there in front of everyone, to thrust my tongue between her plump lips and shiny teeth. Before going to bed I had to rinse my mouth out twice with a mint-flavored mouthwash. I looked at myself in the mirror, gargled, and thought of Daniel Atijas. The first time I had seen him was actually in a photograph on a small poster announcing his talk.

The posters were up, I saw over the following days, on all the Banff Centre buildings, but I had noticed one on the bulletin board by the reception desk when I was waiting for the young woman behind the counter to give me the keys to my room and studio. The bulletin board was plastered with announcements, and the photograph of Daniel Atijas was partly obscured. I only glimpsed it out of the corner of my eye, but that did it. I left the young woman at the desk in mid-sentence, *her* sentence—never would I have interrupted my own—and went over to the bulletin board. Hard to say what I could compare that moment of recognition with, perhaps with the afternoon when, walking along a stream in Kananaskis, I came across a pebble that I still carry with me after all these years. I showed the pebble to Daniel Atijas, when what I was really wanting to do was to hold it up next to his face, though in the end I didn't. So there I was staring at the face in the picture and feeling the tiredness from the morning's early start and all the travel drop away as if I were donning some altogether-new clothes. The young woman tapped me lightly on the shoulder and handed me the keys. I was given a room on the second floor and studio number eight. When she had her back turned, I ripped the poster right off the bulletin board, folded it, and put it in my pocket. The room looked out on the craggy peak of Cascade Mountain. Mountain peaks always soothe me, as if I weren't a person of the plains after all. That was how Daniel Atijas felt, too, he told me as we stood by the window in his third-floor room. At that point I knew much more about him than I could learn from the handful of terse sentences on the poster. I read them only later that evening when I got into bed, the tiredness back: I had spent the whole afternoon at the studio, rearranging the furniture, canvases, and painting supplies, and all I'd wanted to do was to plunk my head onto the pillow and sleep, nothing more, but then I remembered the poster, got up and looked for it in the pocket of the jacket that was hanging in the closet by the entryway, climbed back into bed, switched on the bedside-table lamp, and began to read. Daniel Atijas, it said, is a writer from Belgrade; he has published four novels and two collections of short stories; his work has been translated into a dozen languages; he will be speaking on history and literature in the Balkans; date, time, place. Then I fell asleep. It was two days later that I came away from a conversation with people I knew in the administration with, in my hands, a full file of material on Daniel Atijas: his complete biography, reviews of his books that had been translated into English and French, the transcript of a BBC interview, stories published in American literary magazines, two essays (one, "A Vanishing World"; the other, "Writers and the Collapse of Yugoslavia"), news items on his appearances at various literary gatherings, the schedule for his stay in Banff. In short, I was ready to welcome him, and while I was waiting for his talk to begin, I studied the flakes of dandruff on the shoulders of the president of the Banff Centre. When Daniel Atijas entered the room, I didn't recognize him, so while he was taking his place at the podium by the microphone, I turned, thinking I would catch sight of the Daniel Atijas I was expecting to see as he approached through the rows of seats. Afterward I attributed this misapprehension to my nerves, which kept me from observing clearly, and immediately after that I explained it away as his nerves, which made the lines of his face harsher, and I had to remind myself that photographs always deceive, because no matter how unskillful the people who take them, the pictures always capture what the photographers mean to see through the camera lens. This was June 10. We met on June 11 in the dining hall during lunchtime. Though everything up to that point may have been deliberate, this really was a chance encounter. I was sitting alone at a large round table, poking at noodles I had chosen for no obvious reason, when Daniel Atijas stopped by and asked if there was a free place for him to sit. He was holding a tray with a bowl of soup and a salad. Nobody here but me, I said, and even I am not here at times. Daniel Atijas smiled fleetingly, as if uncomfortable at intruding on my solitude. He struck me as the type who was more concerned about others than himself, but I didn't say so. I waited for him to sit, and then I introduced myself, courteously, slowly, though I still couldn't believe he was sitting across from me, and said, no secret, that I had been at his talk and that I had enjoyed his evenhanded presentation, particularly, I remarked, when he spoke of the interaction, or rather clash, between urban and rural writing in contemporary Serbian literature. Daniel Atijas nodded and started to eat his soup. I couldn't, I said, help but notice that a similar relationship, at times even to the point of intolerance, existed in western Canada—in other words, here, I said, where the rural experience still defines its spirit, though, I said, nine-tenths of the population are living in greater or smaller urban areas. Cities are like women, I said then, but Daniel Atijas only sipped his soup and glanced from time to time out the window. Once he reached for the salad I had almost given up, but I mustered the strength to continue, which did not happen once he'd left, for despite my desire to get up right then and there and follow him out, I could not quiet the trembling of my thighs, and sank back into the chair. The noodles still lay on the plate, the fork groaned under caked ketchup, the spoon was flat on its back, iceberg-like the napkin rose toward my lips. Everything was the same, yet it was all different. The next few days, I carefully studied the schedule for Daniel Atijas's stay at the Centre; I amassed more information, followed his movements, always from afar, kept an eye in the dining room on what he ate and with whom he sat, eavesdropped on conversations two or three times. I felt like a spider spinning its web, not the web of children's stories, of course, which invariably symbolizes something evil, not at all — in fact, spiders are always welcome at my studio in Saskatoon; as far as I'm concerned the spider is a marvelous architect, an artist of space. Were I a spider, my web would have been an artwork in progress — in rapid progress, no doubt, for, judging by his schedule, I saw that Daniel Atijas was going to spend a total of thirteen days in Banff: he had arrived on June 9 and was leaving on June 22. No time to lose, I told my face in the mirror as I shaved the next morning. If I am not mistaken, that was a Sunday, June 14. I was one of the first down for breakfast; Daniel Atijas was one of the last to arrive. Hidden behind a newspaper spread wide, I watched him serve himself scrambled eggs and orange juice. He sat at a table at the other end of the dining hall, where two Japanese women were already seated. They soon struck up a lively conversation, which infuriated me, though I don't anger easily, but after four cups of coffee I was having difficulty sitting still. Several times my feet seemed to be walking away from the table all by themselves. I was beginning to start in again on articles I had already read when Daniel Atijas finally stood. The Japanese women rose and bowed at the same time, and then, releasing me from the horror of the thought that they might all be leaving together, the women sat down. Daniel Atijas walked through the dining hall and up the stairs. I put the newspaper down and went after him. At the exit, however, I lost sight of him, and just as I was about to break into a run, someone grabbed me by the shoulder: Mark Robinson, a poet from Regina. If I had had it in me, I would have decked him then and there—I had never liked his poems anyway—but he was a whole head taller than I, with a broader girth, so I had to allow him to draw me close, press his cheek to mine, and thump me on the back. I, meanwhile, peered over his shoulder in hopes of catching sight of at least a patch of Daniel Atijas's jacket. I regained my composure much later— drinking coffee again in the same building but now at the little restaurant off to the side—when Mark mentioned a party that evening at the home of the director of the Literary Arts Programs, to which all the writers had been invited, he claimed, and I believed him immediately, who were resident just then at the Centre. Thrills shivered through me. Sometimes, I thought, losing sight is better than seeing. And besides, I was acquainted with the director of the Literary Arts Programs, and his wife, what's more, was from Saskatoon, so I was always welcome to show up at the front door and knock, even though I am not a writer and hadn't been invited. All the while I strained to keep all this from showing on my face, but eyes, as they say, are the mirror of the soul, and Mark, whether I liked his poems or not, was a poet nevertheless, and he suddenly looked hard at me and grumbled: You are on to something, admit it. At first I dug hurriedly through my mind for what I could admit—that the Banff Centre president had dandruff?—then I realized the cloaked meaning of his words, and I said there were plenty of hot-looking babes at the Centre this year, no kidding. Sure thing, said Mark, sure thing. I had no idea, in fact, of who was there, because when I hadn't been following Daniel Atijas or inquiring about him, I had been spending every free moment in my studio working at drawing a face that I had been forever seeking. Not just the features, but its shape and the interrelation of the parts, especially where they defied an anticipated symmetry. I shook off Mark Robinson, but before I did, I had to promise that we'd spend an evening getting drunk together—like old times, said Mark—meaning that we'd reminisce about the years we had spent at the University of Saskatchewan at Saskatoon. I went off to my studio, where I stayed until evening, not even taking a break for lunch, obsessed first by new attempts at capturing the shape of the face and then by sketches for my painting A Rainy Day on the Prairie. More precisely, I struggled first with the shape of the face and then with the shape of rain. I have always wrestled with what is missing, and my paintings depict absence rather than scenes of presence—it's just that no one has ever remarked on this. By six I was at dinner. I dined quickly and went back to my room: the party at the home of the director of the Literary Arts Programs began at seven thirty, and I needed time to get ready. Once I was done with the bathing, shaving, hair drying, the choosing of the right lotion and tie, it was eight. I was not, however, the last to arrive. A playwright from Toronto came after me, and then two Japanese women, though not the same ones who had sat with Daniel Atijas at breakfast. When the wife of the Director of the Literary Arts Programs caught sight of me, she shrieked and flung herself around my neck. The director merely extended his hand in silence. He had never liked me, I knew. His wife said that we must get together, that I simply must not leave Banff before I'd been by to visit them one more time to give her the news about every person she knew who was still living on the prairie. There aren't many left, said the director of the Literary Arts Programs. He was from Halifax and had no notion of what "prairie" meant, regardless of my explaining it to him whenever I came to Banff. How heartily he had laughed one summer when I told him that the prairie is just another form of water. When I said this, I did not mean the waves of grain that often show up in Mark Robinson's poems but the geological fact that there used to be a sea here and that a prairie is, in a way, an absence of water, an absence of presence—something along those lines. Anyone who was not born on the plains cannot understand this, his wife said at the time, which was interesting, especially because she and I, from the prairie, claimed also to understand the mountains, but we refused to accept that people who came from mountainous climes could grasp in its fullness the essence of prairie. I wondered what Daniel Atijas would say to all that, and by then the host and hostess had gone off, leaving me holding a bottle of beer, so I decided to go find him. I scooped a handful of cashews from a bowl on the table and set out on the habitual pilgrimage I undertook, whenever I was at the house of the director of the Literary Arts Programs, to a great wooden sculpture of Buddha seated on a lotus leaf, blissfully smiling and fat. They had brought him back from somewhere in Asia, where they had, long ago, spent two years as teachers of English as a second language in adult education classes. Whenever I visited them, I would visit the sculpture, bow to it discreetly, and stroke its rotund belly. I'd read a while ago in a book that this was supposed to bring luck and a windfall, and just then I needed both. The sculpture stood in a niche in the dining room and seemed, as I came over to it, more serious than ever, yet all I had to do was look into its laughing eyes to forget everything. I nodded to it, wondering whether it remembered me, and stroked its belly with my fingertips. Buddha said not a word, but the voices in the living room swelled with noise. Partly responsible for this was the music blaring from the lower level of the house, but the true culprit, I discovered, was Daniel Atijas, around whom a largish group had drawn, including the director of the Literary Arts Programs and Mark Robinson. The noise was actually coming from Mark, whose rumbling was louder than the muffled thumps of bass and drums, but the clamor was also caused by several people, three or four, talking at once. I mingled with them, found a handy angle from which to study Daniel Atijas's face, and did what I could to follow the threads of the conversation—more a quarrel, actually, no matter how many of the words were cloaked in courtesy. Whatever the case, Daniel Atijas defended himself, and they attacked, or rather prodded him to self-defense, raising criticisms and foisting on him impossible-to-meet conditions. Daniel Atijas repeated that the notion of collective guilt was simply wrong, there was no positive experience with such a thing, and the only outcome of insisting on nation-wide guilt for what had been happening was to give those who really were guilty the feeling that as individuals they had been let off the hook and had not just been forgiven but were being encouraged to go right on doing more of the same. The wrongdoers are people, said Daniel Atijas, people with first and last names whose guilt can be proven; one cannot try a community in court, he said, especially because the community is not the decision maker, at least not in situations like the ones we are talking about. No, no, no, rumbled Mark Robinson, that's pure bull, like when people claim that the German people cannot be blamed for Nazi crimes in World War II, that the misdeeds were the work of individuals who can be counted on the fingers of your hands, and over time, fewer and fewer fingers are needed to count them, until it comes down to a single finger, one man, usually dead by then, and since he is dead, he can conveniently be blamed for everything. Daniel Atijas shook his head. History does not tolerate comparisons, he said, especially not ones rooted in prejudice; the saying that history plays out first as tragedy and a second time as farce, that saying, he said, was emphatically untrue, as the events in his country showed: where there was no evidence of farce, historical or otherwise, but only of tragedy. Their voices were by no means the only ones sparring; several other guests were elbowing their way in to voice an opinion. They mentioned the atom bombs dropped on Hiroshima and Nagasaki, de-Nazification in postwar partitioned Germany, the camps for people of Japanese and German background in the United States and Canada during World War II—and Mark snorted scornfully at all of it. Sanctions against a country, said Daniel Atijas, best suit the people in power; the only thing isolation does is boost their position. He couldn't understand, he said, why those who were imposing isolation as a universal solution for all political maladies couldn't see this; and worse yet, he said, is the insistence on blaming a whole population, which is nothing short of covert racism. It has nothing to do with racism, shouted Mark. It has to do with sound logic. Did anyone, he asked, coerce the Germans into embracing Nazi ideology? I know nothing about the Germans, answered Daniel Atijas in a conciliatory tone. He struck me as someone who was averse to conflict and who would do anything to evade it or capitulate immediately if that failed. But only if doing so defuses the situation, said Daniel Atijas when I asked him before his departure whether my impression had been right. If the conflict is inevitable, he would never give up without a fight, and he would even be prepared, he said, to contemplate suicide, because if there was no other way out, then a plunge is better than defeat without a fight. If he knew nothing about the Germans, said Mark, maybe there was something he knew about the Yugoslavs or the Serbs, or whatever the people he lived with called themselves, and could he say, asked Mark, whether anyone had coerced them into embracing the ideology of nationalism, or had they done so all by themselves, of their own free will? Nationalism needn't be a bad thing, said the director of the Literary Arts Programs, barging into the conversation; in Canada we could use a little nationalism, the good kind, of course, he said, because then we would finally see what really makes us what we are or, actually, what we should be. Ah, said Mark, so we would be just like the Quebecers, and that, to be frank, holds no appeal for me. Daniel Atijas asked whether that meant that the Quebecers knew who they should be. They define themselves in positive terms, the director of the Literary Arts Programs hastened to answer, while we define ourselves in negative terms—that's the difference. The difference, again Mark rumbled, is that you from the east don't know who you are, while we in western Canada have no doubts about ourselves. The prairie defines us, I said, and Daniel Atijas looked at me for the first time that evening. He looked at me, he later explained, with amazement, but also, a moment later, with a tinge of tenderness, because, he said, that was the first time he had heard someone prepared to define himself *not* by language, or background, or history, or military conquest; it was the first time, he said, that he had heard someone seek the limits of their being purely in nature, and he immediately thought, he said, that he could have an ally in a person like that if he were in need of an ally, and he wanted, with that gaze, in which amazement gave way slowly to tenderness, to let me know how much this had meant to him, especially here, among the mountains, where he had really never been. Just then our hostess, the wife of the director of the Literary Arts Programs, sweaty and breathless, inserted herself between us with the demand that we all come down to the lower level, where the music, she said, was pounding and the beat was catchy. She pulled at our arms, pushed, nudged, dabbing the sweat from her forehead at the same time, until most of the people around us relented. So Daniel Atijas and I ended up suddenly alone in the big living room. The music was louder, the sound of the bass guitar and the thump of the drum crept into our feet, while quiet spread around us. The tenderness was gone from Daniel Atijas's gaze — it had lasted longer than I could have hoped for anyway — and in its stead dawned curiosity. I reminded him of our first encounter in the dining hall. I'm the guy, I added, who made the claim that cities are like women. Daniel Atijas said that he remembered, but that then, as now, he could think of nothing except how different everything was here from the world in which he lived. He said it was as if he'd come from another planet, not from southeastern Europe. In his world, he said, there is only the present, and in the present one is actually living for the past, which everyone wishes they could change, while here, if he had understood correctly, the present is only an antechamber to the future, and the past, as it should be, is as unchanging as the mountains around us. Or the prairie, I added, for if there is something unchanging, it is the prairie. What followed was a rambling conversation about nature, about a soul driven to despair by a longing for change, about love from afar, Chinese and Western astrology, the sacred sites of the Native Americans, the *slava* celebration as the crux of Orthodoxy among the Serbs, painting techniques, postmodernism, the cuisine of India, Borges's Aleph, Wittgenstein's fragments, Beckett's silence, Leonard Cohen, Bob Marley, the day when all this would seem like a dream. Whether or not you were dreaming, said the wife of the director of the Literary Arts Programs when she crept up behind us, obviously having caught a few of our last words, I want you to be wide awake tonight and dancing. She grabbed us each by the hand and drew us toward the stairs leading down to the lower level of the house. Here we parted ways: our hostess took Daniel Atijas off to a corner where Mark Robinson and the two Japanese women were bouncing, and I was grabbed, as it later turned out, by a poet from Calgary, whom I immediately loathed, though it was hardly her fault that there was no way I could see Daniel Atijas between the sweaty heads and waving arms. I used a moment when someone was changing the tape or record to thank the poet for dancing with me and went up the stairs and out the door. The night was clear, the sky full of stars, the mountain peaks pale in the moonlight. At the fence by the front gate, as if waiting to come in, stood three deer. They call them elks, I told Daniel Atijas the next day, or wapiti, which in the language of the Aborigines means "white" or "whitish," and that is usually the color of their rumps and little tails. They wander around Banff, I said, like the sacred cows of India, but when they are provoked, I said, they can kill a man. I am like that, too, said Daniel Atijas. I am white, he said, I wander around Banff, and I have a nasty temper; the only thing I'm missing is the tail. Did that mean, he asked, that he might refer to himself as a wapiti? We had finished our descent down the steep path by the cemetery and were on our way along Lynx Street. That would be something to ask an Aborigine, I said, but I doubt they'd call a white man by the name they use for a noble beast, and while we're on the subject of beasts, I said, we should first visit the Museum of Natural History. I had intended to play the role of guide that day and take Daniel Atijas through the most important buildings and parks in Banff. The Museum of Natural History is the place I always liked the most, so I suggested that it be our starting point, but had I known then of everything that would transpire and what sort of complicated trajectory this would propel us along, I would have taken him somewhere far, far away, maybe to the other side of town, or high into the mountains to a lake, though I'm not sure there is a distance or an altitude that can alter fate. I did not know all of that then, I knew nothing at the time, and I was the first to step into the building, which felt pleasantly cool after being in the June scorcher outside. I paid the entrance fee and immediately steered Daniel Atijas to a glass display case of stuffed birds. There was a long-eared owl I wanted to show him, but he was drawn, as I had been when I first visited, to a group of mountain goats and sheep, and almost like a child, he pressed his nose to the glass to have a closer look. After that we visited the gray wolf, the buffalo, the bat, the golden eagle, the swan, and the hummingbird, and Daniel Atijas told me that the collection reminded him of a similar natural history museum in Belgrade, which he hadn't thought of for years, and, come to think of it, he hadn't been there for ages, for so long, in fact, that he wasn't even certain whether it was still up and running, but when he'd last visited, probably on a school trip, he had wanted to stay there forever, and had even cooked up a scheme to hide in a corner somewhere because he had been so moved by the beauty of the animals and saddened, he said, by seeing them in such an unnatural setting, as they were at this museum, stuffed like so many empty sacks and before that, of course, slain by human hands. We went up to the second floor. We stopped before a display case with a lynx and then, in awe, went over to the grizzly. When we turned to look at the collection of fossils and minerals, we breathed a sigh of relief. And when we passed by what had been the office of a former director of the museum, now itself an exhibition space, and a display case with a musk ox, Daniel Atijas stopped before glassed-in shelves on which documents about the history of the museum were laid out. Never during all the years I had been coming to Banff had I even glanced at them, because I have never believed that history lies in documents and archival material and yellowed photographs. But Daniel Atijas was, by all accounts, different. Perhaps this is why he writes and I paint, and besides, history must be much more akin to the relation between word and silence lying at the heart—this I can surmise—of literature than to the relations between forms and volumes lying at the heart—and this I know—of the fine arts. Whatever the case, Daniel Atijas stopped before the glassed-in shelves; for a time he didn't move at all, and when he finally did, he said: Ah, I see. And added: Things never begin in a single point; a beginning must be an array of points. Then straight to my face he said: A single point means staying put; movement begins when the points proliferate. Had he not looked so much like someone who is not given to ranting, I really would have thought he'd gone mad. He saw that I hadn't understood, and he drew my attention to the guest book that was open, propped against a corner of the shelf, and pointed to a specific name at the bottom left. It was someone's signature, a little smudged in spots but legible. Ivan Matulić, it read, and next to that: Globetrotter from Croatia. And then came the date, June 22, 1924. The signature was beautiful, flowery, quite distinct from the indifferent signatures of the American tourists that followed, but it told me nothing except what was obvious at a glance: that many years before, also in the month of June, a man from Croatia had visited the spa at Banff. The ornate signature, I said, would give one to think that he really enjoyed his time at the hot springs. No, said Daniel Atijas, his enjoyment and the hot springs were not what mattered; what mattered was that Yugoslavia had already been a country by then for five or six years, yet this man was not disposed to refer to it as such and instead wrote that he was from only one part, which for him, for Daniel Atijas, was conclusive evidence that things were already beginning to unravel even before they had properly come together. From this very spot, he said, perhaps from right where we are standing, he said, stretches one of those lines, which, when sufficiently taut, he said, pulled the country apart as if it had never been there to begin with. He would not, however, he said, want me to think he was now going to moan and groan; the wheel of time is a primitive device, and unlike all other wheels, it can turn in only one direction, forward, but he could not, he said, resist the allure of speculation, of imagining what if this or that had not happened— for instance, what if Ivan Matulić had written "Yugoslavia" in the book instead of "Croatia." A word created the world, and a word can destroy it, he said, as the kabbalists knew full well, and every lapse is costly, so when Ivan Matulić, probably without a second thought, wrote what he wrote, he gashed the soil of Yugoslavia, which never later healed. Who knew, said Danijel Atijas, that he himself would take such a long trip only to arrive where he'd begun? Symbolically speaking, of course, he said. He was not so crazy, though he might seem crazy, as to claim that the collapse of Yugoslavia had begun in Banff on the slopes of the Rocky Mountains. Misery and defeat so coursed through him that this was the first time I thought of reaching out and touching him. There are diseases, he continued, that we never recover from; they stay inside us, he said, as a necessary counterbalance to health, and as time passes, he said, we become more and more convinced that without it, without the disease, we would never be well, and so it was with him, he said: he was carrying within him his former country like a kind of troth, like a disease that kept returning, though now, he said, he knew that the country had been condemned from the start to a fragile existence and that one day, sooner or later, it was bound to fold. He gestured toward the glassed-in shelf and said that he held nothing against Ivan Matulić; for that matter, he envied him for having been in Banff so long ago, at a time when there must have been fewer tourists and cars and, he assumed, more, many more, birds and wild beasts. I know a host of facts about the development of tourism in Banff, but I felt this was not the right moment to share them, and I could see that though Daniel Atijas seemed to be regaining his composure, it was only a mask that would drop from him with a thud as soon as he was by himself. So I suggested that we get a cup of coffee somewhere and take a break, remarking that many people's first visit to Banff leaves them feeling irritable, unaccustomed as they are to the rarefied, dry air, and that this irritation is, in essence, exhaustion, but they don't realize it. Daniel Atijas wouldn't hear anything of the sort and demanded that we keep to our plan, which we had spent a full two hours mulling the previous evening at the small bar in the Sally Borden building. The plan had, of course, been my idea, and it was designed so that Daniel Atijas would spend almost a whole day with me, touring the museums, galleries, bookstores, and historical monuments, but now I was prepared to give up on all of that, which I told him, despite the anguish with which I uttered the words. Fortunately, Daniel Atijas was more stubborn than I. If the plains connect us, he said, we won't allow mountains to keep us apart. We went outside. The heat was waiting for us like a trusty dog. Daniel Atijas's lips were chapped from the dry air, and from time to time he would peel off crisp flakes of dry skin. We walked in silence among the conifers, carefully dodging bird and deer droppings. Sometimes, said Daniel Atijas, he felt like an animal from a zoo or a nature reserve, particularly when he had a chance, as he did now, to travel somewhere, because all the years spent more or less in isolation must have left their mark, and that, in his opinion, was the main reason he had reacted with such passion. In a way, he said, he was forever choked by the feeling that he didn't know how to behave properly; bereft of all contact, he had lost nearly every chance of comparing himself to others, to the rest of the world, yet, he said, every time he was in a new setting, he could not fend off the impression that everyone was watching him as if he were a sort of weird beast, staring at him, he said, sometimes with curiosity, sometimes in disbelief, and sometimes with unconcealed hatred. Finding oneself in a disconnect like that, he said as we were coming out onto the riverbank, a person cannot maintain his balance forever, and sooner or later, sooner more often than later, he will begin to stagger, and ultimately, he'll fall. Before he came to Banff, he said, he had been in a permanent state of free fall; he could barely stand on his own two feet. The last time he'd walked upright had been three or four years ago, during demonstrations in Belgrade, but now that he was here, he said, he was feeling again that he had a spine, that he was standing on his feet without teetering, without a nagging sense of doubt, without a hunched back, which was probably, he said, owing to life in the mountains, because the mountains force you to always gaze upward at the peaks, to throw your head back until something clicks in your neck, to think of courage, ascent, risk, challenge. I felt I should rise in defense of the plains and said that things aren't so bad on the plains, either, and that a person can also lift his head skyward there, especially at night, when the heavens groan under the weight of the stars. Daniel Atijas accepted this, but quickly added that the difference lies in having to fling your head back to see the peaks when you are in the mountains; when you are on the plains, you can look straight ahead, be indifferent, yet still see sky—and stars, he added. He asked me what the name of the river was where we were standing, so I told him it was the Bow, but I didn't know why, just as I didn't know who had named it. Sometimes remaining nameless is better, I said, because then every name can be yours. Daniel Atijas agreed, or at least I thought he did, for he didn't say anything and went on staring at the facing riverbank. The river was shallow, quick, and, as we found when we crouched and dipped in our fingers, very cold. It is time, Daniel Atijas said, for us to keep moving. He shook his hand and flicked drops of water in all directions. We followed the same route back among the conifers and, by the animal droppings, crossed the street, where again I tried to persuade him to call it a day and have a cup of coffee, and we turned into Bear Street, which took us over to the Whyte Museum. Here on the wide steps I made a new mistake, without meaning to, of course, but a mistake it was, and once it was made, nothing else mattered. So, while we were on our way to the entrance, I recalled that a man I knew, Guy Fletcher, worked at the museum archive, and that he, as I immediately told Daniel Atijas, might know something about that Croatian globetrotter. Back when Ivan Matulić was signing the guest book at the Museum of Natural History, I said, several tens of thousands of tourists were already coming to Banff every year, but probably there had not been many Croatian globetrotters, and if anyone knew all the big and little secrets about Banff, I said, that would be Guy. We stopped on the wide steps, and Daniel Atijas tried to dissuade me from approaching Guy, but I persisted, convinced that this would help me win him over. In fact, it was how I lost him, though I only discovered that later, just as we understand most things in life too late, usually when nothing can be done to change them. We found Guy Fletcher in his office, where all the furniture, even the chairs for visitors, were under piles of newspaper clippings, documents, photographs, files, and bound volumes of newspapers and weekly magazines. Guy listened attentively to our story. Daniel Atijas allowed me to do the telling and spoke up only to correct my faulty pronunciation of the Croatian globetrotter's name. Incredible, said Guy Fletcher when I'd finished, really amazing. He cupped his face with his hands and shook his head. I have been working here twenty-five years, he said, and in twenty-five years no one has inquired about Ivan Matulić, and then, he said, these last ten days the man had been all he heard about, as if there were nothing in the history of Banff but this globetrotter from Croatia and his book. When he saw our surprise, Guy explained that Ivan Matulić returned to Croatia after completing his travels and published several books in Croatian about the peoples he had met and the regions he had traversed, and one of the books, he said, was *Among the Mountains and the Indians: Sketches from Western Canada and the Rocky Mountains*. Guy couldn't, he said, read what Matulić had written, but he'd found an interesting photograph in the book which showed the author admiring a Native American decked in full native dress, replete with a feather headdress, and the Indian, he said, was none other than Chief Long Lance, or rather, he said, the purported Chief Long Lance, for no one was sure whether Long Lance was a genuine Indian, or, if he was, they couldn't say how aboriginal he was and to which tribe he had belonged. He had the book here, he said, but though he searched everywhere, he couldn't put his hand on it to show us, which was not surprising in light of the chaos that reigned in his office, but what was most interesting, he said, was that only ten days or so ago, he had gone through everything, he said, that they had in the archive about Ivan Matulić, and even went, he said, to the Museum of Natural History to photograph the page in the guest book on which one could read quite nicely, though it was slightly smudged, the man's ornate signature. And whence, asked Daniel Atijas, this sudden interest in the Croatian globetrotter? Guy Fletcher said he wasn't interested for his own sake, but had received a call from a man who had introduced himself as Ivan Matulić's grandson and asked to see what there was about his grandfather in the museum archive. Guy couldn't remember the man's name, but somewhere, he said, he had jotted it down, and now he had no idea where to look. From the man, he said, he had learned of the book, and he had asked him for a copy, which the man, the grandson, had immediately agreed to provide, for Guy Fletcher had the impression from the story that Ivan Matulić was one of those eccentrics who had contributed to the prestige that Banff enjoyed today. People, he said, did not come to Banff to be what they were but what they were not; they came to be different, something they could not be wherever they were when they were not in Banff; and by all accounts, he said, this Croatian globetrotter was, indeed, something in Banff that he had not been elsewhere, for Guy had gathered not only from the photograph in the slim volume that had been published years before in Croatia but also from what he had heard from the grandson when he finally brought in the book. Daniel Atijas made no effort to conceal his surprise. This man, he said, this grandson, came all the way from Zagreb just to bring you a copy of his grandfather's book? Why all the way from Zagreb? asked Guy, surprised. Whatever gave him that idea, and why would Ivan Matulić's grandson be coming here from Zagreb anyway? It turned out that the grandson lived in Calgary, where he had been born and where Ivan Matulić had shown up at some point in 1951—or perhaps a year later, as remained to be seen—said Guy, and he could easily ascertain the year had he only a little more time available, two heads, and six extra hands. The grandson's father, he said, meaning Ivan Matulić's son, came with him, or perhaps arrived a year or so thereafter, which also remained to be seen, but for that he'd need a third head, and an extra pair of legs would not be remiss. The whole story was complicated, he said, or at least so it seemed when the grandson tried to tell it, and he was sure of none of it, except that the first time the grandson came, the grandson never looked him in the eye, which says a lot more about a person than all the words he does or does not say. A person who averts his eyes, said Guy, fears disclosing something he carries within him, or, even more often, he fears the possibility that his eyes will give easy access to his soul. Here I had to jump in because I knew Fletcher well, and I knew that *his* eyes were always open wide for anyone interested in a guided tour of *his* soul, and there was a good chance that he would draw Daniel Atijas into an endless tale of how the plane of Guy Fletcher's soul and the plane of Banff converged, regardless of what or whom he was talking about. We're running late, I said to Guy. Gotta go. Daniel Atijas did not hide his displeasure. I was not aware that we were keeping to a set schedule, he said once we were outside again on Bear Street. The sun was high in the sky and the shadows very short, but long enough to hide his eyes, sunken deep under his brows. He struck me as the type who doesn't hold a grudge, but nevertheless I didn't dare risk it, or rather I wasn't *willing* to risk it, so I went back to ask Guy Fletcher to make an effort to retrieve the scrap of paper on which he'd written the name and telephone number of Ivan Matulić's grandson and to let us know immediately once he had. I left him our room numbers at the Banff Centre, and stuck a Post-it note with our numbers to the monitor of his computer. Daniel Atijas was waiting for me in front of the museum. Had I known how much his silence would hurt me, I never would have interrupted Guy's story, but it was too late now, and all I could do was to walk in silence next to him and hope we wouldn't run into anyone from the Centre, because that, I thought, I would not survive. Clouds hurried across the sky, and the two of us hurried through a town where nobody hurries, not the people or the cars or even the Japanese tourists. Everything is slow in Banff; at times it is all like a slow-motion movie. Perhaps it is the altitude; or maybe the rarefied air or the cramped space gives an illusion of size when one is moving slowly through it, so our amble, whether we wanted it to or not, wouldn't last long. Daniel Atijas was soon out of breath, and his lips were parched. He wouldn't want me to think, he told me later when we got back to the Centre, that he was angry at me, because such a thing hadn't occurred to him, and if he was angry at anyone, he was peeved at himself, at his inability to wrench free of the sticky tentacles of history, to elude their foul stench,   · for history, he said, always manifests itself as a stink that becomes noxious in the places where the sedimentation of history is great, and no amount of excavating, either real or spiritual, could get rid of it. This was how he had been living, he said, for the past dozen years, from the moment hostilities erupted in his country and history was flung in everybody's face like a cream pie. No matter how many times he wiped his face clean, he said, some-thing sticky was left; it was as if, he said, everyone could see the stain, even here, thousands of miles from the frenzied mob. There is, however, something even worse than spreading stench, I said to calm him, and that is the places where there is a lack of history. I had America, of course, and Canada, in mind; where we were, I said, in Alberta, white men showed up less than two hundred and fifty years ago, and the first thing they did was to erase the existing history, to turn the fullness into a void, and then, or so they imagined, to impose their own history, but the wound, I said, the wound of that void, had never healed, and therefore their pathetic history, pathetic compared to the one they had destroyed, went on forever in a vacuum with no support, no underpinnings, and one day, of this I was convinced, I said, their history would sink back into that earlier history without a trace, without a sound, as if it had never been here at all. Daniel Atijas replied that he liked that image of cataclysm in which, if he had understood me correctly, the wellspring of the new world order would morph into an underground river, but he doubted that such changes could take place over a short period of time. We were sitting on the terrace by his room, looking out into the night. And besides, what we know, he said, we know only in part; something always eludes us—the impact of a detail or the meaning of the whole, whatever—there is always something missing, and as the years went by, he said, he was more and more inclined to think that the image of Sisyphus pushing that boulder to the top of the hill in vain was the most apt way to show the pointlessness of human existence. What could I say? I told him I was a painter, not a philosopher, and that I saw the world as a delicate play of color and volume, and that I further believed that each of us was seeking something that would allow full appreciation of this give-and-take and thereby, ultimately, an understanding of the world. I fell silent, waiting for him to ask me the inevitable question, and when he finally did ask what I was after, I did not hesitate. I said: Love. He turned slowly to look at me. Now there is a pointless search, he said, for if there is something that does not exist, it is love. I asked him how he knew, barely able to stop myself from reaching out and laying my hand on his arm, pale in the darkness of the night. That is what the books say, he said, though he didn't have, he said, any particular book in mind, but in most books—he believed that all books were written for love—we were trying to reach love through writing, and if there really were such a thing as love, he said, there would be no need to write, there would be no books. We live, he said, in a world that cobbles together or pushes us to cobble together what it is that we are missing, and once we succeed, he said, the world sweeps it away in a flash just so we'll take on yet again the futile effort of retrieving our paradise lost. I was not sure I had understood him, nor was I sure that being understood even mattered to him. He struck me as the type who makes more promises than he keeps, though I thought right away that this was not because of him but because of what other people were thinking or expecting and that he was not necessarily betraying himself but them and their expectations, for which he, of course, could in no way be responsible. I thought of this later, when, after leaving his room, I decided to go to my studio rather than back to my room. The night was dark, and the squinting lamps along the path that led among the studios did not provide much safety. I didn't know what elks do at night, but I hoped that none was sleeping in the middle of the path. Once in my studio, I switched on all the lights, spread out my many attempts at capturing the shape of the face, and compared them for a long time, adding a new line here and there, a little shading, a curve, or a blank space. I couldn't imagine how Daniel Atijas would react were he to see all the sketches, but I knew I could show them to him only if I were satisfied with what I was after. He had expressed a desire several times to see what I was up to, for he could not, he said, imagine me painting, the very image eluded him, and whenever he thought he might be on the right track, I'd say something, he said, that would show him he was way off. It eluded me, too, I said, but I promised him right away that one day I would definitely show him the paintings I was working on, though there weren't as many of them as there were sketches of his face, which pushed me to again postpone displaying them and promise myself that I would give more time to the paintings, or at least to my preparations. I had come to Banff with ideas about big formats, and I would be able to start and finish them only once I had set down, in my mind and on paper, every detail. And so I sat and pored over my stabs at capturing the shape of the face I had always been carrying inside me and imagined myself working on something entirely different, something that would free, not enslave, me, as I had been enslaved, no doubt, by the rash statement I had made that evening that love was what I was after in order to grasp the system of the world. Love, of course, is not received; love is given; only a person who is able to give love has the right to get it; he who is only seeking it while giving nothing of himself to others has nothing good to hope for. I had failed to say all this to Daniel Atijas, and it was too late to remedy the situation: midnight was long since past. I was fidgeting in my studio, indecisive and anxious, surrounded by drawings and sketches, and not a single trustworthy word came to mind. Later I recalled a little gesture of his, the tip of his index finger running along the curve of his eyebrow, and that helped me feel more confident, though I still kept opening my mouth like a fish. Anyone seeing me would have thought I was yawning. My jaws hurt so badly from doing this that in the end I had to take two aspirins and lie down on the little sofa under the window. Here I fell asleep and had a funny dream in which the president of the Banff Centre was giving a long-winded explanation about how a space that is too cramped and a space that is too expansive can both shape a person's soul: the first imposes constraints, so he feels limited and uninterested in pain, whereas the second disperses him, thereby stripping him of his true sense of proportion and all support. And a soul with no support, said the president of the Banff Centre in my dream, is condemned forever to free-fall. Meanwhile he kept brushing the dandruff from his shoulders, then clapping his hands, and the dandruff would waft haze-like into the air. Lucky thing, I thought, that I am not dreaming about his wife, and I woke. I picked up a pencil and added a few lines to two sketches of the face. If my calculations were correct, Daniel Atijas would be leaving in seven days. One always counts the days and skips the nights, I thought; I'd have felt better saying: Daniel Atijas is leaving in seven days and six nights. That would have come out sounding like more, longer, though ultimately his stay would end no matter what, and the nights could change nothing as far as that was concerned, whether they were counted or not. Night did not exist for Daniel Atijas. He was, he said, a daytime person; for him night was only a lead-up to day, a time to wait for light, because without light, at least for him, he said, he couldn't accomplish a thing; he couldn't even think, let alone write, and so he always wrote during the day, in early morning or early evening, hence at a time, he said, when the light was gathering or slowly dispersing and when contrasts became, first, in the morning, sharper and sharper and then, at twilight, less and less so. If it were up to him to use a single word to qualify his prose, he said, though he really hoped no one would ever ask him to, but if they did, he said, if someone asked for one word to capture his prose, then the word would be: "cross-fading." That did not, of course, he said, mean an ordinary shift from one form to another, and he certainly was not thinking, for instance, of Escher's geometric metamorphoses, or a butterfly emerging from its cocoon, or even Dalí's surrealist landscapes, but of that essentially inexplicable shift from idea to thought and then to the spoken and written word, of the very moment when nothing becomes something, flying in the face, he said, of all natural laws. With that, he said, he associated dawn and dusk, times of tender renewal and subtle separation, when the darkness turns into particles of light and then light turns into dark dough. We talked about that on a day when we went off for a walk along the river to have a look at unusual rock formations along the riverbank. For us these are only geological forms, I said to Daniel Atijas, but for the Native Americans they are giants who come alive at night and heave boulders at the people who, whether by chance or intent, have gone wandering among them. Daniel Atijas wanted to know exactly what the giants were called, and I had to repeat the name several times: hoodoos, hoodoos, hoodoos. Hoodoos, said Daniel Atijas. Yes, I said, we would describe the hoodoo as the result of erosion, the effect of water and wind, while for Native Americans, as with all else in nature, they were yet another life form. For me, too, said Daniel Atijas, and that is when he launched into his story of dawn and dusk, transformation and cross-fading. For me it's different, I told him, because for me everything needs to be measured and outlined with precision — there can be nothing without edges. I have to know, I said, where one thing begins, whatever it may be, and where the next thing, whatever it is, ends. The world is a mosaic, I said, and every stone is distinct, yet meaning accrues only to the whole. Outside the whole, I said, each little piece is nothing, or, at best, an enigma. Or a secret, said Daniel Atijas, gesturing at the hoodoos, just as these formations are a secret, or an enigma, because if we declare them to have come about by happenstance, we strip nature of all its meaning, which, he said, sounded undoable to him, but if we call them a secret, or perhaps an enigma, then we are fully equating nature with sentient beings just, he said, like us. I stopped and asked whether he was sure he had come from the plains, because I found his thinking so startling. He answered that he most definitely had; he was from the region of Vojvodina, which is actually a southern stretch of the Pannonian Plain, which used to be covered, long ago, by sea, and where the Romans, the

Huns, the Ostrogoths, the Slavs, and the Avars, among others, had lived, while today Hungarians, Serbs, Croats, Slovaks, Romanians, Ruthenians, Romanies, Jews were living there, so the ferment begun in the sea depths hadn't stopped, he said, on dry land. But, he said, he wasn't sure why his remarks had startled me, for he felt that in me, since I also came from a place that had once been a sea floor, he had an ally, and he even saw in me, to be frank, a kindred spirit such as he hadn't encountered in some time. My heart pranced, my eyes welled with tears, but I pretended nothing was happening and stared fixedly at the rock figures. I had something different in mind, I said, the fact that on the plains most people do not see beyond the perimeter of their property, and anything that begins beyond where their field of wheat or rapeseed ends doesn't exist for them. One might expect plains to expand one's horizons, but instead, I said, they shrink them, circumscribe them, impoverishing a person to the extreme, limiting him to only as far as he can see, so the person of the plains, I said, is always at a loss, regardless of where he happens to be. Mountains, on the other hand, I said, mountains are strange, and instead of imposing limits, they are the most freeing, so a person of the mountains, who surely must have his limitations, has more breadth than a person of the plains, which at first glance sounds highly illogical and which no one would ever say, I said. He himself certainly would not have said that, said Daniel Atijas, because he had always been convinced of the exact opposite, and he even mentioned an Austrian writer who wrote dark books about selfish and narrow-minded Austrians obsessed with prejudice and who kept repeating that this was all because they lived in mountains, while he, he said, could think of no one who had written anything like that about people from the plains. This is not proof, of course, he said, but it sounds pretty convincing, with which I had to agree, especially because I couldn't come back to him with any examples from the history of painting; I could only say that there were many fine artists who had left behind them paintings of plains and mountain peaks in which there were often human figures, but these offered no hints of the impact that the plains or mountains might have had on the figures or whether those from the mountains would have been depicted differently had they been shown mid-plain, or vice versa. I asked myself that same question at the studio late that night, the same night I dreamed of the president of the Banff Centre. I was looking over the sketches and drawings, adding a line or shade in places, and wondering whether everything would have been different had I met Daniel Atijas on the plains, in Saskatchewan, and whether the endless breadth of prairie would have made the features of his face, in that earthly sea, crumble and blanch like animal bones. Outside, day was already breaking, the birds were starting to chirp, a squirrel scampered across the roof, and when I opened the door, I saw an elk sniffing the branches behind the neighboring studio. I went off to my room, took a shower, resisted the temptation to lie down again, sat in an armchair to wait for them to start serving breakfast, and here I was woken by the ringing of the phone. It was nine sharp, and at first, as I lurched out of my dream, I didn't recognize Guy Fletcher's voice. I've found it, he said. I had no idea what he was talking about, I couldn't even figure out how to tell him so, but the words slowly moved into the right places and finally I remembered what it was he was aiming to say. He had found, he said, the slip of paper with the name and address of Ivan Matulić's grandson, and not only that, he said, he hadn't stopped there; he went right ahead and called the man, which was, he said, last night, as soon he had found the slip of paper, which, until that very moment, he had been absolutely convinced he would never lay hands on. In brief, he said, Stephen had agreed to come and meet us, and that is what he wanted to let me know, why he'd called, and it's not that he had waited this late to call, he said, no, he had tried to find me the night before, but no one had picked up, not even at midnight, so, he said, he had begun to fret, for the number of tourists over the years who had miscalculated how far away something was or who had come too close to a cliff edge was not small, and had I not picked up the phone this time, he said, he was poised to call the police, but now he was relieved, he could feel himself regaining his composure and feel his good mood returning, and now he could, he said, await Stephen's arrival calmly, which they had set for two in the afternoon, and after that, for instance at four, we, Daniel and I, could meet up with him, he said, but before he was able to continue, I quickly thanked him, confirmed that we would be waiting for Stephen at four out in front of the museum, and hung up. Daniel Atijas, however, did not come down to breakfast, or he might have gone before I got there, nor was he up in his room when I knocked a little later at his door. I scribbled a message on the back of an old receipt and pushed it under the door. Banff is not a large town, and the Centre is even smaller, but when you don't know where to look for someone, size is moot. I glanced into the restaurant, walked through the gallery, went to the beginning of the path running by the cemetery: nowhere did I see Daniel Atijas. I returned to the tennis court, went down to the Sally Borden building, leaned on the railing of the little terrace, and peered through the glass wall of the pool. Two women were floating in the water, two men were dozing on deck chairs: none of them Daniel Atijas. I left and set out up the hill toward the wooded area where the studios are. At the beginning of the path between the clusters of the practice huts for the musicians I stopped and listened for a few minutes to the muted strains of a cello. The sun was already high in the sky: it was looking as if today would be warmer than yesterday. The cello fell silent, and when it sounded again, I crossed the little wooden bridge and headed toward my own studio. If nothing else, I thought, at least I'll be able to get out of the baking heat. In my message to Daniel Atijas I had written that I would be in my room at three, and if he hadn't turned up by then, I would be waiting for him at four in front of the Whyte Museum, and I reminded him to wear a hat and bring lip balm. I could have written so much more, since he struck me as the type who pays no attention to his needs, someone who is heedless of himself, though I also knew I should tread carefully, for he also looked like the type who does not like to be told so, and who in his apparent, or perhaps genuine, neglect sees a kind of attention. This attitude sounds complicated, but it was simple—much simpler, in any case, than my efforts to find the right line for the right face in the space delimited by the perimeter of a sheet of paper. I entered the studio, put water on for coffee, took out the file with the information about Daniel Atijas, spread my papers and photographs around on the floor, stood up, sat down, stood up again, flipped open a sketch pad, poured the coffee, sat again, arranged the photographs in a series, arranged the drawings in another, shook my head, rubbed my face, propped my elbows on the edge of the table, and when I looked up at the clock, it was already noon, nearly twelve thirty, so there was still time to hope, to fend off despair. After all, even if Daniel Atijas had not shown up, if he had perhaps gone with someone to Calgary, which would have been ridiculous in the extreme, since Ivan Matulić's grandson was on his way from Calgary to Banff, even then I would have gone to the museum alone, though, to be frank, I didn't know what I would have had to say to this grandson or how I would have kept him there until Daniel Atijas showed up. I went on shuffling through the papers on the floor. Of the four stories of his that I had, I knew two nearly by heart, one of them I didn't like, and one I didn't understand at all. In the story I didn't understand, made up of four long fragments, a young writer, never named, wakes up in the middle of the night after having a dream in which he has clearly seen and read the best story that could ever be written, but when he wakes up and sits at his desk to write it down, he makes no headway. What he writes is more like gibberish than a story, and after many attempts,

42

which turn his entire life into a futile stab at re-creating the story of his dreams, he finally recalls the first sentence—and instantly loses all desire to write any further. This is the gist of the first fragment. In the second, the world has stopped turning; the whole cosmos stands still; eternal day begins on one hemisphere, eternal night on the other. No one pays attention, but when the temperature starts rising on one hemisphere while steadily dropping on the other, chaos ensues, about which the story says, "Never, especially now, have there been any words that would suffice." The fragment ends, "In any case, we did not vainly believe in silence." The third fragment was a meticulously kept record, catalogue-like, of a young woman's stroll down a main street in the pedestrian zone of a large city. She goes down one side, then crosses over and comes back to where she started. Along the way she stops at every shoe store—there are nine of them in total, four on the first side, five on the other—and in each of the seven store windows she sees at least one pair of shoes dear to her heart. She pays no attention to any of the other stores, except a kiosk where she purchases cigarettes and a pack of condoms. In the last fragment, the longest, the writer appears again, but this time he is old and decrepit; he can barely remember the titles of the books he has written, and when he does remember, he is no longer sure what they are about. Outside it's night, late, but he cannot fall asleep. "He stopped sleeping," the story reads, "a long time ago" and sits out on the terrace of his apartment above the main shopping street in the town where he lives. The sky above him is dark, and the darkness may be as dense as it is precisely because the street is brightly lit by the reflection shining off the store windows, particularly the stores where they sell Italian shoes. "If this were a dream," thinks the writer, "and if I were to wake up now, maybe I would be able to write the world's best story." But no matter how tightly he shuts his eyes, he cannot make himself fall asleep. This is how the story ends, though it would be better to say that here it only begins. No matter how I tried, I wasn't sure I had understood it fully; no matter how many threads I found among the fragments, I still had the sense that the central thread was eluding me; no matter how I tried to discover the right pathway between the many layers of waking and sleeping, at the end the story left me beyond its perimeter, as if I were a person knocking at an open door, able to glimpse a slice of the scene inside but lacking the strength to push open the heavy door and enter a space that might be himself. Who knows how many times I had read the story over the past five-six days. I never asked Daniel Atijas for its true meaning and probably never will, because I knew what he would say—the same thing I say when asked a question like that: artists do not explain, they create. For an artist to start explaining his work is a sure sign that something is wrong. Faced with a work, why should we believe words about it? And when a work is fashioned of words, that is when one should least believe the words, for if the work does not speak outside the medium in which it was created, then it is stifled and constrained by its physical qualities. Worst of all is when I hear people speak of the "masterful strokes" of my brush, when critics hold forth on the way I apply paint, as if the painting is nothing more than canvas, paint, brush, and frame. So when they ask me, I say nothing, I am at a loss. Someone will say I am no good at speaking, but this is not true. The only thing I desire is not to explain my painting in words, because I haven't conceptualized it in words. A painting begins as a painting, in images, just as a story, I presume, begins as a story, in words, though not in the words themselves but in the spaces between, somewhere between silence and articulation. A story is not a simple collection of words, just as a painting is not a simple collection of visual elements. And a painting, one could say, comes about in the space between the images. Our works, I said to Daniel Atijas one evening, exist precisely because there are always those blank spaces between the words, between the visual forms, and when the day comes when the interspace is filled, writers will stop writing and painters will jettison their paintings and drawings. He merely shook his head and, addressing no one in particular, including me, said that the apocalypse never comes alone. I turned to look at the door of his room as if the apocalypse were in the doorway. It wasn't, just as there was no one, a moment later, at the door to my studio when, driven by the thought that someone was knocking, I raced over to open it. I stepped outside and looked down the path, then up it. Near the neighboring studio I saw a squirrel, that was all, but squirrels, which may be aggressive, have not yet reached the point of knocking on people's doors in search of hazelnuts and peanuts. I went back into the studio, fiddled with rearranging a few of the pages and two-three photographs, then put everything back into the file and briefly focused on the drawings, adding yet another line, not entirely necessary but still appealing, and then I slipped them quickly into the sketch pad. Three o'clock arrived very soon, and it was high time for me to be off. I waited until almost three thirty: the phone didn't ring, no one knocked, no one called my name, and soon, when there was not a moment left to lose, I had to go back along the same path, the one that ran by the cemetery, where I had once tried to explain to Daniel Atijas that some people are forever outward bound, as was he, while others are forever inward bound, as am I, though I didn't tell him that part at the time. I went down Wolverine Street, cut across Grizzly, went through a few back alleys and then down Buffalo, and headed toward the river and the Whyte Museum. I don't know what I was expecting when Guy Fletcher informed me of the meeting with Ivan Matulić's grandson, probably nothing, for meeting him held no interest for me, but even had I harbored any expectations, the man I saw waiting in front of the museum steps could not have met them. I didn't think this because he was small, gaunt, with sunken black eyes and thin lips, but because of the layers of grief or a similar emotion that were dripping off his face, which he made no effort to conceal. I couldn't say that he was relishing the grief or similar emotion, but it was clear, or so it seemed to me at least, that the pain didn't bother him, and that, as an attitude, had always bothered me. I went over, introduced myself, and said my acquaintance was running a bit late, I was sure he would be here shortly, and we could see where to take it after that. The grandson shrugged. I didn't know what more to tell him, and he, obviously, didn't know what to ask me. So there we stood on Bear Street watching the tourists and the cars and then staring at a robin working a worm up out of the soil on the lawn out in front of the museum. Just when it had tugged out the worm, nearly tipping over onto its back in the process, Daniel Atijas appeared. The worm has nothing to do with it, I said to the grandson as Daniel Atijas was approaching the museum, though one never knows for sure, and who knows where my friend would be now had the worm stayed stuck in the ground. The grandson shot me a baffled look. He had no clue what I was talking about, and he did not, as I saw, realize that Daniel Atijas was heading toward us for he didn't know Daniel Atijas; he had never seen him and probably wouldn't even know his name. Perhaps, at the end of their meeting, Guy Fletcher had told him to step outside, that there would be two men out in front of the museum who would like a word with him. The grandson was indecisive at first, for he had counted on getting back to Calgary as soon as possible, but Guy Fletcher was adamant, persuasive, chatty, and the grandson stayed. Guy Fletcher was relieved, I was sure he was, when all that grief left his office. He sped to the window, cranked it open, and took a deep breath of the warm, dry, heedless mountain air. I couldn't blame him, if that is, indeed, what he did, for that much grief, or whatever it was on the grandson's face, might choke an unwary onlooker, and having in mind what it felt like here, where we were standing in the open by the river, I could only imagine its horrific effect indoors. Later, however, when the three of us, Daniel Atijas, Ivan Matulić's grandson, and I, were indoors, in

Daniel's room, I noticed that my misgivings had been unwarranted. The grief was still there on the grandson's face, but by then, if I can put it this way, his was only half the grief: the other half had sidled over onto Daniel Atijas's face. And while the grandson's face slowly began showing a softness I had seen no trace of earlier, Daniel Atijas's face, at least for that evening and night, looked less and less like the face I had been drawing and because of which I was sitting where, by all accounts, I should not have been. The next day during breakfast I tried to explain this to Daniel Atijas through the haze of his and my hangovers, but my mouth was dry, the words stuck to one another, and I had to give up before I'd properly begun. Daniel Atijas kept shaking his head, stopping only long enough to sip his coffee. We held our coffee cups like drowning men clinging to life belts. He had thought, said Daniel Atijas finally, that he would not be able to fall asleep last night at all, but as soon he dropped his head onto his pillow, he sank into a deep, though unfortunately not refreshing, sleep, which was probably, he said, obvious, and me? he said, asking how long I had slept. I said that, unlike him, I had dropped off to sleep while my face was still in the air above the pillow and that I had slept, if my arithmetic wasn't off, at least four, maybe five hours. I don't know why I had to lie and why I didn't admit that I had slept on the floor next to the bed and that when I woke, I couldn't get back to sleep afterward, in part because of what all of us, and particularly Daniel Atijas and Ivan Matulić's grandson, had talked about, and because of my fear that Daniel Atijas's face wouldn't go back to being the way it had been before, but also because of everything that had been playing out inside me, about which, even if I'd wanted to, I couldn't have spoken. I woke up at four; the sky by then was starting to fill with light, and soon the light was so bright that I could no longer squint it out, so I got up and watched the morning turn into the world. Excess is never a good thing, said Daniel Atijas, regardless of whether it was excess of drink, food, music, or whatever else. Last night, for instance, he said, we gorged ourselves on words, and if we had vomited later, if we could have, out of us would have gushed half-chewed, gnawed words, jumbled sentences, the occasional punctuation mark. Both of us raised our hands high—he his left, me my right—to flag down the waiter and his jug of coffee. At noon we were supposed to meet again with Ivan Matulić's grandson; instead of going back to Calgary he had gone to spend the night at a cousin's in Canmore about twelve miles from Banff; at the very thought of the words we'd be saying then, though most of them would belong to Daniel Atijas and the grandson, I began feeling queasy, though, like every addict, I could hardly wait to feel that way. The waiter finally came over, poured coffee into the cups shaking in our hands, tsk-tsked, and promised he'd be back again soon whether we hailed him or not. Daniel Atijas's face was once again the face I had seen on the small poster by the reception desk. True, tiredness had left its mark, his eyes had shrunk, the corners of his lips were loose, but all that, I was convinced, was transitory, and none of it alarmed me. What did alarm me was something I sensed more than saw, something which still had no definite shape, nor was it attached to any particular part of his face, something which, at least for the moment, I would not have been able to draw but which kept slipping, shadowlike, over his features, his brow and the bridge of his nose, threatening, at some point, to stop and stay, I feared, for good. It was not, to be frank, the shadow itself I feared, its density or its reach; what worried me was that in it I saw only a beginning, an intimation of events that had been set in motion and could no longer, as in a Greek or Shakespearean tragedy, be recalled. I am a child of the plains and don't know much about avalanches, but while we were sitting that morning in the dining hall of the Centre in Banff waiting for the waiter to bring fresh coffee I could not suppress the thought that we were in the path of an avalanche from which, no matter what we did, we would not escape. I didn't even try to explain this to Daniel Atijas, and had I tried, I wouldn't have gotten it right, but even if I had gotten it right, he wouldn't have believed me—this I know. I later wrote on the back of a drawing that it was interesting that I felt no jealousy at all, which was unusual, since Ivan Matulić's grandson attracted Daniel Atijas in a way that I had not; something had sprung up between them that I could not touch, a rapport they shared through their background, even though Ivan Matulić's grandson, as he had told us the previous evening, was born in Canada, whereas Daniel Atijas was a Jew, an outsider, essentially, in the place where the grandson's ancestors were from. In that sense, "background" is the wrong word, but better that word than none at all, though I doubt that Daniel Atijas, as a writer, would agree. Whatever the case, they had spent yesterday and last night growing closer and closer, not along a straight, one-way trajectory, but rather along one full of small retreats and advances, as if they were playing chess on an invisible board with invisible pieces. At first, of course, it looked as if they wouldn't even shake hands, let alone sit at the same table, and I even thought, watching the restraint with which the grandson greeted Daniel Atijas, that this was all wrong and that the grandson—and I was prepared to bet on it at the time—would soon be on his way. I reckoned that Guy Fletcher must have told him something, who knows what, for nothing else could have explained the grandson's reticence. The next morning while we were at breakfast, actually while we were holding our cups of coffee, Daniel Atijas explained that coffee drinking was a ritual that now marked, without fail, every encounter between people from his former country, especially if they were in enemy camps, regardless of whether the person was someone who actually lived there, such as Daniel Atijas himself, or a descendant, such as Ivan Matulić's grandson. All this, said Daniel Atijas, flagging down the waiter, is inevitable, and understandably inevitable at that, he said, for time is remembered, in the words of a poet, as a series of segments strung between wars, as a series of time markers—before, after, during the war—and therefore those who share war, he said, feel greater affinity than those who share peace. And greater distrust, he added a little later, when I'd already assumed he would not be speaking again, for he, he said, was from Belgrade, the capital of Serbia, and Ivan Matulić was from Zagreb, the capital of Croatia, and, he said, the greater part of the war went on in a conflict between Serbs and Croats, from which neither of them, though one was a Canadian and the other a Jew, could escape. Short on sleep and long on caffeine, I could accept that explanation calmly, but the previous evening I had not hidden my surprise and dismay. Ivan Matulić's grandson had shown, of course, typical western-Canadian politeness, but this was only a façade. I believe that Daniel Atijas could feel it too, but he never, not even for a moment, betrayed himself. He walked to the grandson's right and I to the grandson's left, and spoke as if the existence of the world depended on what he would say. They spoke in English, though not so much for my sake as for the sake of the grandson, for his Croatian, he said, had been reduced to everyday niceties, stock phrases, and, of course, swear words. That is how it started: with a story about language. We had strolled around the streets of Banff talking about language and the identity problems of first- and second-generation immigrants, along the way settling on where we might go for dinner. Daniel Atijas mentioned local specialties, Ivan Matulić's grandson was all for Ukrainian, I was up for sushi. In the end we went to The Coyote's Den. The grandson had grown gentler by then; his face was fuller, his answers longer, and his questions less frequent. From that moment until about midnight he addressed me more often than he did Daniel Atijas because he was talking about things that I, he believed, could understand. And I did. All of us in Canada, after all, were immigrants, some earlier and some later, with only a handful of people, five-six hundred thousand Indians, who could claim to have come from here, who really belonged to country and clime, so the story of Ivan Matulić's grandson, the first part of his story, actually, was very familiar. In order to give voice to everything that was bothering him, said the grandson, he would have to start from the middle and move forward and backward in time, sometimes in space as well, though that shouldn't worry him, said Daniel Atijas, as there are stories that can be told only that way. There are those, he said, that have to follow a linear sequence, in which what follows cannot be told before what precedes it, just as there are those, he said, which should be told backwards, starting from the end, though he always felt, he said, that the best are those which, like the grandson's, start from the middle and then, a little like a tangled skein, resist anyone's predictions about how they will unravel. We kept walking along the main street, on the stretch from Buffalo to Wolf, because this is where the restaurants were that we had been debating about. The grandson's story had not begun until we stepped into The Coyote's Den, though he had already been talking for nearly an hour. Two or three times till then we had stopped so that they, Daniel Atijas and the grandson, could settle a difference, but nothing grew out of it; even when they raised their voices, it didn't seem to become a point for serious contention. First there was talk of language, of that double world, the twofold microcosm of new immigrants from which, said the grandson, when he'd finally left his family home, he came out dazed, split in two, as open as a seashell but also glad, he said, that at last he was on his way to becoming whole, complete, alone — and he was not shy about saying this. First of all he stopped eating any kind of Croatian food, for there was nothing quite so awful, he said, as when he'd come home from school, open the front door, and be assaulted by the smells of food, after which he would sink back into the Croatian language in a world in which there was simply nothing else. He didn't know, he said, whether he would be able to explain this clearly, but sometimes because of being split this way he thought he was losing his mind. The front door to his house was like a magical gateway, he said, because on both sides of it there was a reality that was unreal in terms of the reality on the other side. He wouldn't want someone to think, he said, that he didn't love his parents or his grandfather, but while he watched his friends at school his only thought was how he wanted to be like them, living in only one language, in a body that wasn't cleft in two. When he came home from school, he'd see his grandfather snoring on the living room sofa, his mother's mother, a kerchief over her hair, fussing in clouds of steam over pots and pans and brandishing a wooden spoon, and he would start thinking right away about how to be as different as possible from them. He remembered, he said, how at the time he longed to be an astronaut, who could live, he earnestly hoped, in outer space, far from his home in the northeastern part of Calgary. At that point we were already sitting at a table in The Coyote's Den having a beer. Daniel Atijas had raised the issue of multiculturalism and embarked on a long sentence, but both Ivan Matulić's grandson and I almost simultaneously broke in, claiming that what we were talking about, or what the grandson was talking about, had nothing to do with multiculturalism. The world either opens or it closes, I said, and that is all that counts. Multiculturalism is an ideal, said the grandson, which is not doable. Living in layers, I said, doesn't work. Or being in two places at once, said the grandson. Daniel Atijas looked first at him and then at me and asked why the two of us had attacked him in unison. He smelled a conspiracy, he said, and in that case, the best thing would be to order another beer. He turned to look for a waiter. I had nothing against beer, I said, nor was this a conspiracy of two Canadians against a Yugoslav, but he, Daniel Atijas, I said, had touched on a painful nerve in our society, and we, I said, nodding at Ivan Matulić's grandson, were compelled to react. Daniel Atijas said that now he was really confused; he had always assumed that the politics of multiculturalism were the best way of overcoming and eradicating differences. Oh, no, I said, multiculturalism actually exacerbates differences, even making them insurmountable with its pointless insistence on the fact that everyone is sufficient unto him- or herself and that traditions should be preserved in a vacuum beyond the reach of other influences; yet the only way to survive, I said, which is true for the whole living world, is to mingle: there is no other way. The waitress brought three steins and set them in the middle of the table. We clinked glasses, drank in silence, then licked the foam from our lips. Only our table was quiet, of course, for The Coyote's Den, as always during the summer months, was packed. We could hear words of Dutch, French, and Japanese, as well as strains of a song that German tourists were drunkenly singing. Don't get us wrong, I said to Daniel Atijas, or rather, I corrected myself, don't get me wrong, because it is difficult enough to speak in one's own name, let alone for someone else, especially, I said, when you don't really know the someone else. Multiculturalism, I went on, has its good side, too, and if one takes into consideration the long tradition of British, and white men's, racism in Canada, then the introduction of multicultur- alism as an official state policy is entirely justified, but in the end, if multiculturalism has no other objective than continual self- affirmation, then it turns into a kind of soft racism, stripped of the violence, rage, and polemical overtones. I sounded silly to myself as I said these words while the German tourists were vying to out-yodel each other. Daniel Atijas took another sip of his beer, licked his lips again, and said that he had believed his whole life that multiculturalism was the pinnacle of societal achievement and that it was what had made him glad to be living in a country such as Yugoslavia. But, Ivan Matulić's grandson interrupted, it was precisely the collapse of Yugoslavia that showed that the policy of multiculturalism led, in extreme cases, to inflaming dif- ferences until they became irreconcilable. Besides, he said, if there was someone who should be disheartened and dismayed, then that should be he, for he, and he could say this to us now, had done his part to bring about the downfall of multicultural- ism. A small part, true, he said, but sometimes a single grain of salt is all that is needed to disturb the equilibrium and send a wave hurtling outward, destroying everything in its path. The German tourists had stopped singing and were studying the bill the waitress had brought them. Daniel Atijas stared at the grand- son, and for the first time since we'd met, I couldn't read precisely which it was in his gaze, hatred or pity. Who knows, my gaze was, perhaps, giving off something similar, so I made an effort to look at no one, nothing, not even the beer mug. I had needed ten days to work out a strategy and elaborate all the details for how I might get close to Daniel Atijas, yet Ivan Matulić's grandson had come closer to him, I could feel it, in less than three, or was it four, hours. Even if what I had sensed was hatred, it was a hatred that attracted, unlike the hatred that might have been in my gaze, and which belonged to that more sincere variety, a hatred that raises obstacles, that is capable of murder. I would have given anything, I thought, to be back at my studio just then, focused on the face as never before. Later, of course, I regretted even thinking of hatred, but at that point it was too late to do anything, and it seemed somehow unjust that I be the only one to come away from it all unscathed, so I brought the almost-forgotten hatred out, which until then I had suppressed under the clamor of German yodeling and shouting, and cloaked myself in it as if it were some sort of cape which I wear to this day. All of this is now moot, of course, like the countless other things that at one moment mean so much to us, yet later, after only a few minutes, we can no longer understand how we could have paid them—the thing or person, regardless—so much attention. Later, much later, I realized that, albeit unintentionally, Ivan Matulić's grandson and I had confronted Daniel Atijas with challenging dualities: light versus darkness; here a door opening, there a world closing; first a hush, then silence. But the road to silence always traverses noise, and so we, too, had first to suffer with the commotion at The Coyote's Den, then the crowds at The Sailor's Pub, until finally, taking shortcuts and back alleys, we came out on the path by the cemetery along which Daniel Atijas and I had come into town, except that now we were climbing it up to the Banff Centre. We went to Lloyd Hall, veering around three little dark mounds, which we were convinced were three slumbering deer, and went up to Daniel Atijas's room. By then we were very drunk, we staggered and propped each other up, and later, when Daniel Atijas took an unopened bottle of whiskey from his suitcase and placed it on the table, the night turned into a series of fragments with blunt edges between which there were blanks. I woke up in my room on the floor by the bed, fully dressed. I didn't know how I'd gotten there, how I'd left Daniel Atijas's room, what had happened to Ivan Matulić's grandson. All I knew was that every movement, even the slightest, made my head fall to pieces and then, in some magnificent way, reassemble itself. The red light on the phone was blinking, a sign that someone had been looking for me and, not having found me, had left a message. I thought, of course, of Daniel Atijas, then of the grandson, and then, though I tried to fend it off, of Mark Robinson and the director of the Literary Arts Programs, but I could not bring myself to press anything, even the telephone receiver, to my temple, though if I had rested the phone on one of my big ears my ear would have held it far enough away from my skull for comfort. The light blinked, and slowly, as if in a slow-motion film, I moved from lying down to sitting. I rested for a moment and then managed to stand, though only for a second, because I had to sit right down again on the edge of the bed. If someone had suggested just then that I should lean over and look under the bed, I thought, I would have punched him so hard that I would have knocked all his teeth down his throat. This was pure exaggeration, for there was no way I could even lift my arm, let alone get the momentum going or direct a blow to a specific spot. But suddenly I thought that maybe this was exactly what I should be doing, that I ought to lean over and look under the bed. If I had turned up next to the bed without knowing how I'd gotten there, mightn't there be someone underneath it? The light kept blinking in closer and closer sync with the pain pulsing in my temples, the back of my head, my neck, and it made no difference at all whether I was watching it or had squeezed my eyes shut. Slowly, quite slowly, I crouched, then kneeled with my palms on the rug. When I tried to bring my head to the floor, keeping my balance by thrusting my bottom into the air, the blood rushed so violently into my temples that it nearly toppled me over. There was no way around it: I had to lie back down. Some people are so destined, I said later to Daniel Atijas, no matter what they do, no matter how hard they try, to always end up at the beginning. Daniel Atijas dismissed this with a wave. He was the one who ought to be complaining, he said, noting that at least until he left, there would be no switching of roles; in other words, he was the only real loser, and he would stay that way to the end. But under the bed, when I finally raised the hem of the bedspread and peered into the wan darkness, no one was there. I don't know what I was expecting to find, and probably, consider-

ing the shape I was in, I was expecting nothing. When you con-
tain emptiness, you cannot hope for much better than more
emptiness, though it would make more sense to call this hollowness, for emptiness can be filled, whereas hollowness is what remains when everything else is taken away—the closest description of my state that morning. Emptiness, said Daniel Atijas in
response to this, is the presence of absence; hollowness, he went
on, is the absence of presence. Of course, I replied, though I was
miffed that I hadn't come up with this myself. Ivan Matulić's
grandson said nothing. Maybe he hadn't yet joined us at that
point, maybe it was just the two of us, but that doesn't matter so
much now, even though who is listening to someone's words
always matters, for just as a tree falling, unheard, in the woods
makes no sound, a person who is speaking only to himself is not
actually speaking to anyone; he is silent. All I had left to do, I told
Daniel Atijas, was to stand, which I finally did after who knows
how long, and then, just as I was, at last, on my feet, the light on
the phone stopped blinking. I suddenly remembered everything
that Ivan Matulić's grandson had been talking about, though I
couldn't decide whether it was at The Coyote's Den or The
Sailor's Pub, or in Daniel Atijas's room. I remembered how at
first I had listened to him with a little smile, the way we usually
like to show the person speaking that we are, genuinely or otherwise, interested in what they are saying, and how that smile
began to fade. Actually, it froze, then it changed into a grimace,
so all I could do was cover it with my hand and, using my fingers,
poke downward at the corners of my mouth. I remembered how

at one moment Daniel Atijas plunged his face into his hands as if to bury it and how I noticed then for the first time that his hair was thinning. And I remembered how at one point I thought I didn't want to hear it all but quickly forgot and could no longer summon the thought, so I went on listening until I stopped hearing altogether or until the words turned into creatures of weird shapes and sizes. The beginning of the conversation could be said to be ordinary, as Daniel Atijas immediately agreed. We spoke of language and exile, multiculturalism and life on the plains. Ivan Matulić's grandson said he was proud to be a western Canadian of the second, in fact, third generation, for that was special in a region where white people had been dwelling for only some two hundred and fifty years. From there the conversation touched briefly on the question of the rights of Aboriginal peoples and the tragic fate of Native Americans, but Daniel Atijas showed no interest in this. He declared that he'd had it with all of the Balkan natives back where he was from, he'd had it with depressing stories, and added that there are some who cannot adapt to the demands of civilization, and some cannot adapt to life in a multiethnic community, but as far as he was concerned, both of these were deliberate decisions, made, he said, not as a manifestation of powerlessness, but, to the contrary, as a way of gaining power. Ivan Matulić's grandson went on talking for a while about tragic episodes in the history of relations between whites and Aborigines, particularly about epidemics, some deliberately sowed, that devastated the First Nations in but a few years. We were speaking of that, I am absolutely certain, at The

Coyote's Den, for I remember when Daniel Atijas said that he had never seen a coyote, to which Ivan Matulić's grandson responded by holding forth on the role of the coyote in the folklore of North American Indians, particularly those living in the endless expanses of prairie. In this first part of the conversation, especially when there was talk about the features of western-Canadian identity, Ivan Matulić's grandson spoke mostly to me, expecting, probably, my understanding, or at least my readiness to understand, which Daniel Atijas apparently was not willing or able to show, but once we got to The Sailor's Pub, things changed. This might have had something to do with the beer, the mood at the pub, perhaps the Irish music being performed by a group of young men and women, or perhaps Daniel Atijas deliberately pushed aside whatever had made him so distant in the previous restaurant, but regardless of why, we all became more talkative, we all gestured a lot, shouting over one another and everyone else, pounding our feet to the rhythm of the music, whooping now and then, and guzzling beer, while the whole time, and this is the most interesting part, we were conducting a fragmented yet interlinked conversation about human destiny. Daniel Atijas had struck me from the first as the type who was good at adapting to circumstances even when the circumstances seemed to be adapting him. The talk of destiny, as one might expect from a conversation in a tavern, careered along in free association, reeling from pithy philosophical quotes and paraphrases of literature and artworks to long, free-ranging meditations on the lack of predictability or the predetermined nature of destiny, depending on who was doing the talking. Sometimes the three of us spoke at once, just as we all stopped talking at once a few times. Then I felt an almost-tangible discomfort, for I was convinced that I could see forming between Daniel Atijas and Ivan Matulić's grandson a subtle thread of rapport, something which had never begun, let alone formed, between Daniel Atijas and me. Then we were quite drunk and none of us could say with certainty how many beers we had had. Daniel Atijas claimed we'd downed eight bottles, meaning eight each, of course, but then he shrugged that off, saying that this meant nothing, because numbers were mere conventions; every person, he said, can define numbers for themselves, and he, for instance, he said, might speak of eight empties, all the while having, for instance, sixteen or twelve in mind, or not even one, which would be particularly strange, because zero is not actually a number, since it signifies nothing, and nothing, as everyone knows, he said, cannot be counted. Perhaps things would have been different, said Ivan Matulić's grandson, had we been drinking from steins, though then, he realized, it would have been harder to keep track, since steins, he said, hold more beer than fits in a bottle yet less than fits in two. This shows, said Daniel Atijas, that the differences in the systems of education don't count, because even though there can be no doubt that the European system is more rigorous than the North American system, he said, none of us is able to do arithmetic properly, so it's best, he said, for us to order another round, which will, he was convinced, refresh us and perhaps spur us on in such serious endeavors of thought. The noise at The Sailor's Pub had become really unbearable by then, and for us to hear one another we had to shout into one another's ears, which I had never liked, especially when Daniel Atijas's lips touched the whorls of Ivan Matulić's grandson's ear. He was shouting into my ear from a greater distance, I was sure of it. So I was the first to say that it was time for us to go, not meaning that we should go off somewhere together but that we each go our separate way, though it wasn't late and the night, as we saw when we went outside, wasn't quite dense enough yet; the darkness was more a dark blue than a black. Only when we were out in front of the restaurant, when the freshness of the night made us feel first more sober and then more drunk than we actually were, Daniel Atijas suggested that we all go to his place, to his room at Lloyd Hall, for he had something there, he said, which would make us happy, and happiness, he said, is not something to dismiss out of hand, with which Ivan Matulić's grandson and I agreed. All three of us were swaying, though there wasn't even the lightest breeze, and when we finally made it down Beaver Street to Buffalo and went into the back alley that was paved in gravel, every little stone, even the smallest, was a nearly insurmountable obstacle. Like mountain climbers, we negotiated the steep path that led by the cemetery, one by one, with pushing and shoving, occasional curses, and assertions that the time had finally come for us to seek a place for our eternal rest, for every honest person, said Daniel Atijas, has already lain a long time in his grave, while we, he said, like these phantoms, are flailing about on mountain peaks. When we reached the top of the path, we caught sight of the three little mounds in the dark, and just in case, convinced that they were slumbering elks, we made a large detour around them, which took us to the entrance of Lloyd Hall. While we were going up to the third floor in the elevator I felt as if I were in a boat. Everything rocked and lurched so much that I said so out loud, and Ivan Matulić's grandson replied that perhaps this was Noah's ark, a comment to which Daniel Atijas added that mankind would not have much to hope for if the three of us were the last to survive on earth. Furthermore, he said, Noah's ark had moved along a horizontal axis, while we, he said, were moving vertically; and while Noah's ark conquered space and time, both were inaccessible to us, he said, because in essence, we were standing in place. Neither Ivan Matulić's grandson nor I had anything to say to that, the grandson because he had dozed off, his face pressed into the corner of the elevator, and I because I was thinking that if I were to open my mouth even a little, I would throw up. I relaxed only when the elevator stopped, the door opened, and we stepped out onto the carpeted floor, though I was still pressing my lips tightly together. Daniel Atijas groped for his room key in his left pocket, then remembered to look in his right, where the key actually was. Ivan Matulić's grandson was the first to go into the bathroom, Daniel Atijas went after him, and I after him. Two or three droplets of urine glistened on the floor in front of the toilet bowl, a crumpled sheet of toilet paper floated on the water, a soft hum came from the pipes, and the toilet was groaning like a human being when I pressed the little lever that protruded from the side. When I went back into the room, Daniel Atijas opened his suitcase and produced the bottle of whiskey. It took us a while to find two glasses and a plastic cup, and then time, too, began to disintegrate, and later, the next morning, I wasn't always able to find the right sounds for the images that had been cropping up before my eyes. I would see, for instance, Ivan Matulić's grandson sobbing, or his face convulsing into an awful grimace, but his words didn't reach me, and instead my voice would be monotonously listing the exemplars of prairie flora and fauna, though I don't remember that we had been talking about that at all; or I would see Daniel Atijas, say, shake his head and speak with incredulity while all I could hear was Ivan Matulić's grandson's drunken song, and that in an unfamiliar language. There were, however, also whole fragments, as well as those that, though whole, went on in silence. The only thing lacking was sound fragments in darkness, though that part of the night plunged regularly into darkness and then swam out of it again. Just as the body has no memory of pain, said Daniel Atijas when I mentioned this to him later, so the mind has no memory of darkness. I am not sure that's so, but I didn't want to argue, though I did not fail to tell him that I remember certain moments in prairie darkness and that each of them, each of these darknesses, was distinct. Daniel Atijas was adamant. He shot back that those are later memories and that I, as a painter, strove to discover the nuances in something that in fact had no color at all. Now that I think about it, he had struck me from the very start as the type who can be stubborn, though I had not expected him to be *so* stubborn, which only shows that a person must be considerate of everything, including himself—even more so himself, perhaps, than others, since it is always easier to betray oneself than others. I said something like that, I remember, in the middle of the night, just when Ivan Matulić's grandson was throwing up in the bathroom. Before that, a while before that, he was kneeling in front of Daniel Atijas, hugging his knees and trying to peel off his socks, with the intention, he said, of kissing his feet. As Daniel Atijas was pushing him away, an entirely sober look flashed for just a moment in his eyes, but then it faded, and no matter how hard I later tried, I couldn't find it again. Ivan Matulić's grandson, and I can say this now, looked totally undignified, spittle dribbling down his chin, his forehead covered in beads of sweat, hiccupping and burping and doing nothing to hide it. He mentioned a secret, something about how he had a secret, how he had stumbled upon the secret, but ever since that moment his life had not been what it was before. He was not able, when I asked him, to say what his life had been before, but he was certain that he would never be able to go back to his earlier self, whatever that meant. There you are, he said, walking along one side of the street, and then, after years and years, he said, you cross over, and nothing is ever the same again. Something like that, he said, had happened with his life, too. He crossed over to the other side, and nothing was the same. He could see things he hadn't noticed before, but he wasn't sure he wanted to. Then he went to the bathroom to throw up, and Daniel Atijas asked me whether I played chess. I told him I would have to think about that for a while because I couldn't remember, but by the time I finally recalled some moves and even saw the beginning of the Sicilian defense quite clearly, I heard him snoring. Just then Ivan Matulić's grandson came out of the bathroom, ashen and rumpled, and just in case, though it was obvious that he was spent, I moved my leg to the side. He raised the bottle, held it up to the night light to gauge how full it was, said that there were two fingers left, one for each of us, he said, and tipped back the bottle and drank down his finger of whiskey. Then I drank my finger's worth, and then for ages I held the upside-down bottle over my outspread palm, from which I licked the last drops. I put the bottle down on the table and peered at it, and that is the last scene I remember; it was one of the ones that was going on in total silence, though I am certain that somewhere behind me Daniel Atijas was snoring steadily. I woke up in my room on the floor by the bed, fully clothed. My mouth was dry, my lips chapped and crusty, and with every movement, even the slightest, my head threatened to roll off my neck. I do not know how I got to my feet and made it to breakfast, but to my astonishment Daniel Atijas was already there. He was drinking coffee and eating toast, spread with a thin layer of margarine. He would like to have someone tell him, he said, how long a person can go on remembering a country once it is no longer there. Austria-Hungary, for instance, he said—is there anyone left who remembers it? Is there anyone who misses it still? Not as a historical fact, he said, but as a genuine country or, better yet, he said, a country which had been like a father for somebody, or like a mother, either way? He assumed they would, one day, think of his country that way, too, a curiosity of history, an entity defying historical inevitability, a stage created for great and small wartime events, only no one, he said, will speak of the feelings that used to stir in people. No one cares. People hardly have time for their own feelings, he said, let alone for someone else's, and least of all for the feelings of someone who does not know what he is feeling, for he doesn't know what to relate those feelings to or whether he'd even dare to show them at all, since we all know what people think about those who insist on clinging to feelings that differ from other people's, who are not prepared to accept the new reality, and thereby, he said, are forever reminding others, too, of a reality which maybe never should have been changed after all. He wouldn't want, he said, for me to think he was the type of person who suffers from irrational grief for something that is not there; he wasn't grieving for what was lacking, he said, but for what could have been. He knew, he said, that this was only a trick, a ruse he used to bolster his spirits, which, in his case, he said, was another name for reason, but there were moments when it was only by hook or by crook, he said, that he kept going. And besides, he was well aware that prowess lay not in finding, he said. True prowess lay in losing again what had been found, whatever one had sought for a long time, but, this time, losing it the right way, as Nietzsche had written for his Zarathustra — or was it in another book? he said. Nietzsche's or Kierkegaard's? Who knew, there were so many, one couldn't keep track of them all, and for years now, he said, he had been thinking it would be best, though he himself was a writer, to read only one book per lifetime, and even that, he said, might be overdoing it. Yes, now that he thought about it, he said, a story, one of Borges's, for instance, or, why not, a poem, one of Rilke's elegies, say, would do nicely, especially a Rilke, none of which can ever be plumbed, no matter how many times we read it. I replied that the same could be said for paintings, that there were paintings that could replace entire galleries, I said, and that sometimes it would be enough, or, perhaps, better, I said, to look at this one painting, one of Bosch's canvases or a Dürer graphic, for instance, and not burn oneself out by traipsing through the entire museum, especially since museums are getting larger and their impact is therefore waning, for no one has the stamina to see everything that is on show. And when we stop and think about what will never be shown, said Daniel Atijas, what is stowed away in museum warehouses, only then, it seemed to him, are we forever condemned, he said, to a fragmented being and a fragmented world, to a life that unfolds by sidestepping life. He hastened to add that this probably sounded like the words of an embittered or disappointed person and that he most certainly did not see himself that way, but it was difficult where he lived, given his predicament, to preserve a sense of composure, and even more so, he said, his buoyancy and energy. Where everything was at a standstill, he said, where life was like sludge, everyone was falling apart, no matter how much they were trying to avoid it, to escape the general entropy, by sealing themselves into a hermetic space or in silence—a fitting choice, he said, for a writer. Several years he spent in silence, but he still felt, he said, the moral filth, so sometimes in the shower he would scrub himself for hours in a vain attempt to scrape off the stain he'd picked up from others. He had always felt, he said, that every person is obliged to do all he can do to stand up to moral depravity, but he also felt, he said, that each of us must take the measure of this obligation and decide how to mount their own opposition, for only that way, he said, by bypassing protocol, can morals be defended. There are things to address first in the human soul, he said, and only afterward can we take the barricades into the streets. However, such an attitude had placed him in a situation in which he could never entirely satisfy anyone, for introversion, he said, like every form of silence, can be read two ways, as support or as reproach, meaning that recently he had been forced to put up with pressures from various quarters and to face down demands that he voice his views in public. His whole life, he said, he had been mounting a poetic of silence, and now they were calling for noisy words, and in the noise, he said, he simply could not find his bearings. Someone had once told him that his country, his former country, he should call it, was a botched experiment, so it was to be expected that the country would blow up at some point, as happens, he said, with badly mixed and highly volatile chemical compounds, where one drop too many was enough to blow up an entire lab. This comment deeply insulted him, he said, because he had never, not even now, felt like a lab rat or a guinea pig; he breathed life in deeply, just as people did anywhere. I told him I understood him, for there were times when I was overwhelmed by the feeling that the country where I was living was nothing more than an experiment—an experiment, I said, for which there were no guarantees of success. When I said that I wasn't thinking of Quebec, but of the other parts of the country, the western provinces in particular, which had never conformed to the confederation. And besides, I said, this confederation claimed the equality of its members, while actually it was always asymmetric. The east overshadowed the west, I said, and always they were trying to avoid finding themselves in the middle, and always a supernatural sense for equilibrium was needed to govern such a country, which most politicians, of course, never mustered. Daniel Atijas said he understood me now because if he had been telling my story before, now I was telling his, which only shows, he added, that we can never hope for anything good from history, especially from its repetitions. It's a lucky thing, I said, that the history of his country cannot repeat itself here in its fullness, that there are variations in the repetition, which are essentially the result of an assortment of differences, including different views on society and the world, different frames of mind, religious beliefs, ethnic prejudices, and so forth. Daniel Atijas was surprised. He even said that he could not believe his ears, and to reinforce this he jiggled each ear, first the right, then the left, with a finger. There's nothing to be done about it, he said. It has nothing to do with war; all this showed was that I had no idea what war really is, and that I still entertained romantic notions about war, and that he wouldn't be surprised if, like Heraclitus, I believed that war was the father of all things, the cause and creator of change. Nothing could be further from the truth, said I, least of all the thought that politicians determine when a war begins and how it will go. Even if Quebec were to secede, he said, that would be no reason for war, but when the first inhabitant of Anglo-Saxon background has to leave his country because of pressure from French nationalists, then, he said, war will be inevitable. And what will go on between the new, independent Quebec government and the First Nations living on Quebec territory? About that, he said, he didn't even dare think. About that, to be frank, I, too, did not dare think, but I didn't want to say so. And besides, we had already been sitting there too long, drinking coffee, though, if nothing else, at least we no longer looked as if we were drowning. Daniel Atijas's face had back its natural complexion and had freed itself of its phantom pallor, while my cheeks, I could see in the mirror that covered the wall behind his back, were flushed with color. We left and stood for a while out in front of the building in the warm rays of the afternoon sun. The fragrance of pines was in the air, a swarm of tiny flies hovered high above us, an elk was dozing on the grass across from us, sounds of a ball thudding against a racket at regular intervals came our way from the tennis courts, someone behind us spoke about the weather forecast, which included rain and possibly sleet, and I suggested to Daniel Atijas that we spend the time, until Ivan Matulić's grandson arrived, at the Walter Phillips Gallery, where we could avoid, almost entirely, I said, the pressures of external sensation, reducing them to a minimum so we could recover. Daniel Atijas shrugged and came along. At the entrance we found a sign saying there was an installation on exhibit in the gallery of "New Work" by Argentinian ceramics artist

Anna Maria Corazón, which very nicely, I said, suited our feeling of revival after a drunken binge. In the middle of the main room there was a large clay plateau like one of those mesas in Arizona and New Mexico, and in its middle, lit by a powerful beam of light from the ceiling, was a lake filled with real water. The water flowed out in four directions and poured down the rim of the mesa, dividing it into four equal parts. At the bottom the water flowed into a channel surrounding the mesa that, when the circle was nearly complete, became an underground river. Here, I assumed, the water went into a hollow place beneath the mesa, from which it came up again, probably with the help of a pump, and poured back into the lake. Around the mesa, organized in a pattern that I could not divine, there were other island-like structures, filled with a large number of fantastical creatures, plants, and buildings, which a person, I thought, would need five or six months, if not more, to study carefully. We sat in chairs placed by the entrance and gave ourselves over to the burbling of the water. There are people, said Daniel Atijas, who still believe in new worlds, which is, he added, just a little pathetic, though comforting, too, given the times we live in — times in which, for certain, there are no new worlds to be had. I tried to counter this, but benignly, as much as the circumstances allowed, saying what I believed — that every artwork is, in fact, a new world — which would mean, I went on, that new worlds would continue appearing as long as there were people under the sun who created things. Daniel Atijas made no bones about masking the grimace of disgust on his face. Today's artists, he said, are not much more than motes shed by the original trees, by the colossi that artists used to be. It used to be that the finest artists were like giant sequoias, he said, towering above everyone else, but today, in the best of cases, they are no more than dwarf pines and cannot see themselves, let alone others. We, he said, are now regressing, and this, for certain, is a period of backward movement, like many others in human history, no doubt, but never has one lasted so long, nor has one offered us so little hope of radical change. This, he gestured toward the ceramic installation, is admittedly a consolation, but that is all that is left to us, consolation. We can hope for little else. His head dropped to his chest, his eyes closed, and I thought he would fall sleep, but then I saw that his eyelashes were fluttering and that he was peeking out beneath the lids. Maybe it wasn't such a great idea for us to come to the gallery, I thought, because the coolness coming from the air conditioners refreshed the spirit and then dulled it, and the stimulating effect of the caffeine was slowly wearing off while its diuretic effect was becoming more pronounced. A dark-haired woman stepped into the gallery. She had on a dress with a flowery design, her hair was done up in a ponytail, she was in sandals. She went over to the mesa, crouched, and dipped the tip of her right index finger into the stream. Did he have any idea, I asked Daniel Atijas in a whisper, why Ivan Matulić's grandson had spoken so often the night before of a secret? Daniel Atijas said not a word. The woman stood up, circled the mesa, stopped in the same place, crouched again. And did he know, I went on whispering, how I got to my room? Without standing up, the woman looked at me over her left shoulder. With her right index finger she again touched the surface of the water. Daniel Atijas softly smacked his lips. The woman stood up and stretched, and for a moment her arms, out-stretched, and legs, akimbo, described an almost-perfect letter X. Then she left. Daniel Atijas was convinced, he said a few minutes later when we went out after her, that she was the artist who had made the installation, and he could readily imagine, he said, the horror she must have felt when she came into the gallery and saw that there were only two discombobulated visitors there. Had I ever, he asked, sat in a gallery during one of my own shows and waited to watch the gallerygoers? And what did I then, he wanted to know, expect to see? He, he said, was appalled when-ever he saw one of his readers. He of course had nothing against readers, he said, and in fact, he wasn't at all concerned about them, but some of the people he saw, especially some of the women—no, he wouldn't wish readers like that on anyone, not even on the writers of socialist realism. I continued to be inter-ested in how I had reached my room the night before, but Daniel Atijas avoided answering, claiming that it wasn't that he was avoiding an answer but that he did not know. Perhaps Ivan Matu-lić's grandson, who'd be arriving shortly, would be able to help, said Daniel Atijas. The only thing he knew, he said, was that at one point he'd noticed I was no longer there, but he couldn't re-member whether Ivan Matulić's grandson had said something to him, which didn't need to mean anything, because it was quite plausible that he hadn't asked him anything. Words by then had become as heavy as sandbags, he said, and every time he tried to speak, he had the impression that his tongue might snap off. At the thought that Ivan Matulić's grandson and he had been alone together *after* my departure, no matter what had transpired, everything inside me snapped. I staggered, and if Daniel Atijas hadn't grabbed me by the elbow while at the same time opening the gallery door, I would have gone straight through the plate glass. I am certain of it. As it was, leaning on his arm, I managed to stay upright and stepped bravely out into air that, though warmer than it had been inside, was actually cooler, at least for me. It seemed, remarked Daniel Atijas, that neither he nor I was fully sober yet, for everything had been rocking back and forth for him a moment before in the hallway; for a moment he'd felt as if he had been standing still while everything else moved around him, but then he looked to his side, he said, and saw me, and everything somehow reverted to normal. He began walking again, keeping step, and again everything settled back into the way it was supposed to be. The sense of stillness couldn't have lasted long, he said, but he knew this would be one of those moments he would never forget, that surge of certainty when he observed my steady pace, when he saw my eye blink. Interesting, he said, that in life it is often moments like these, apparently so trivial, that we remember more than we do the grand adventures or major thresholds, which last longer. It's as if our consciousness, he said, no matter what that consciousness might be, accepts that a grain of sand means more than a whole desert, that in one grain of sand all the other grains are hiding; he who recognizes the grain, with his heart, if possible, can then understand the desert, he said, even if he has never set foot on it. I wasn't sure how to understand these words, just as I wasn't sure whether they had anything to do with me, and what—if they were referring to me—was implied by "grain" and what by "desert." Was Daniel Atijas speaking of love or devotion? Was there a difference? Whatever the case, I knew from that moment on that there was something that could serve as consolation, and things are always easier to take with consolation, even the least likely sort, than without it. When I think of his earlier words, I feel that Daniel Atijas would have approved if only I had asked him. I did not, however, say anything. We stood next to each other on the little terrace out in front of the restaurant, and while Daniel Atijas squinted and basked in the sun, I was fidgety with restlessness, clinging to my fragile consolation. Later, when we came over to the staircase leading to the entrance to the dining hall, we caught sight of Ivan Matulić's grandson. While I was watching him, hunched slightly over, walking along the path that ran from the parking lot, I promised myself that I would be courteous and that I wouldn't say anything I might later, ever, regret, but I did not succeed, I admit, in fully suppressing the malice I felt when he had almost reached us and I saw that his face was showing traces of the events of the night before: the bags under the bloodshot eyes, the ashen pallor, the visible wrinkles. It did not, of course, occur to me that I might look the same, just as Daniel Atijas did, after all, and that the malice belonged to all of us at once and to the same extent. I mustered the stamina to greet Ivan Matulić's grandson with a smile, and then, looking out of the corner of my eye while being extremely nonchalant, I paid close attention to how Daniel Atijas and he greeted each other, what they said, where their hands were, and, in the end, whether they were arching their eyebrows as a sign that they were overjoyed at seeing a person they cherished. Ivan Matulić's grandson was, in fact, quite restrained, and it was easy to see that he was being cautious when we began talking about the previous night. It turned out that each of us remembered the night as a sequence of blank stretches between which events played out that at times made sense and that at others were extremely cryptic. So Ivan Matulić's grandson knew how I'd made it to my room, a trip of which I knew nothing; Daniel Atijas knew exactly when Ivan Matulić's grandson sat in his car and, despite his drunken state, drove off toward Canmore, while the grandson remembered only the driving but not the instant when he took his seat in the car or the moment he got out of it; I remembered when Ivan Matulić's grandson tried to kiss Daniel Atijas's feet, which neither of them recalled and which neither really cared to recall. When he had gotten tired of hearing me say over and over that I was going to die or some such nonsense, said Ivan Matulić's grandson, he resolved to take me to my room, no simple task, he said, for first he had to figure out where my room was, but once he'd extracted that information, he said, the journey was not so arduous, certainly not as difficult as the effort he'd had to invest in working out how to keep the door to Daniel Atijas's room from shutting while he was taking me, because he could not, he said, get the key from Daniel Atijas, who was snoring loudly and refused to stir, no matter, he said, how hard he tried to wake him, as, God knows, he did. In the end he jammed a slipper under the door, though he fretted the whole time he was going down in the elevator and as he rode back up whether he would find the door shut, which would have meant, since Daniel Atijas was sleeping, that he would not have been able to get into the room, but everything worked out fine after all, or rather seemed fine until he brought me to my room, where I thanked him for his efforts in the most ordinary voice, as if sober that instant, entered the room, and shut the door, but when he turned to go back to the elevator, he heard a crash and, assuming I'd fallen, came back to my door, where, after knocking softly and calling to no purpose (he had to keep in mind, after all, the rules of good behavior, which meant that he couldn't kick the door with all his might or holler my name, though even that wouldn't have helped much, he believed; indeed, it wouldn't have made a whit of difference), he, after the soft knocking and calling, finally went back to the elevator, glancing over his shoulder as he went, and rode up to the third floor, where his concern for my welfare, he said, gradually gave way to anxiety about the stability of the slipper under the door to Daniel Atijas's room, and luckily—for had the door slammed shut, he said, he really would not have known what to do—luckily the slipper was where he'd left it, just as Daniel Atijas was where he had left him, having moved only a little. Daniel Atijas raised his head and asked where I was, but before Ivan Matulić's grandson was able to tell him anything, his head dropped back onto the pillow, and back to sleep he went. In short, I could breathe a sigh of relief, but I was still wondering, though I didn't dare ask, what happened later while he and Daniel Atijas were alone, between the time when Ivan Matulić's grandson returned to the room and the time he left for Canmore. Knowing of our memory lapses, I could readily assume that everything proceeded in that blurred state between waking and sleeping, though I still quaked, in part because nothing is less sure than human nature. Rare is the person who can keep his pledge to the end, whatever the pledge may be, and I saw no reason why Daniel Atijas would be any different, nor, after all, was I. In the end, Daniel Atijas had no obligation to me, and if there ever was someone who did have an obligation, then that was I, except that the obligation was not so much to him as to myself, which comes down, in extreme cases, to the same thing. As to the question of lunch that one of us had raised, Ivan Matulić's grandson said he would not be able to even think of food for days, and as far as he was concerned, a bowl of soup would do just fine, though now that he was thinking about it, tea would suit him best. Daniel Atijas chimed in, adding that it would be nice to have the tea elsewhere because he was getting sick of the dining hall at the Banff Centre—not the facility, he added, but the atmosphere, the smell of food that seeped into everything, and the excited voices of the hungry people, resonant at first and then, as the lunch proceeded, duller and duller, less and less vibrant, until finally there was nothing left but a swallowed yawn and a yen for a nap. He knew, of course, that the atmosphere wasn't a question of choice, it was a physical inevitability, but ever since he had become ac-

quainted with the habits of northern Europeans and their prefer-
ence for a main meal in the evening, closer to the time one re-
tires yet not so close as to disturb their sleep, which, as he had
seen earlier, was how Canadians and Americans ate as well, he
had become so partial to that dining schedule that he had given
serious thought as to whether it might have shaped relations between the north and the south, thinking, of course, of the south
of Europe, the Mediterranean, where people are known to take
every opportunity to nap and sometimes spend more time asleep
during the day than at night. There could be no question but that
the north was more advanced than the south, and not only where
Europe was concerned. Elsewhere the north was advanced,
while the south was mainly in disrepair, and this encouraged him
in his conviction that there ought to be in-depth research done
into the nutritional habits of southerners and northerners across
all the continents, including Africa and Australia. Such a de-
tailed study, he said, might entirely uproot the assumptions we
have about the purpose of meals and sleep, meaning, in other
words, that the final outcome might completely change the way
people think about themselves, and change the world. One never
knows where the turning points are, where the lever of change
rests, he said, and we seldom, if ever, recognize turning points
when they appear but only later, once the change has irreversibly
begun and we are surprised by how we failed to spot it, or, con-
versely, we pretend we did notice it, but this is usually an out-
and-out lie. Now, he said, in his country everyone is saying that
from the start they knew what would happen and where things

were headed, but the truth of the matter is that ten years earlier no one had had any clue as to the degree of horror, devastation, and human degradation that would one day be deemed history. Most of us, he said, lag behind life and never really catch up. One might say, he said, that we trail after it, forever late for what life is all about—in which case, he said, we should snap to it and get that tea before someone else drinks it. Ivan Matulić's grandson chuckled. Daniel Atijas only shook his head. There is no better place in Banff for tea, I said, than the restaurant at the old Banff Springs Hotel, and so we sat in the grandson's car, drove into town, crossed the bridge, and drove along the other bank of the Bow River. I remarked how odd it was that no one had taken Daniel Atijas there yet, for going there was usually the first thing visitors did in Banff, so I regaled them until we got there with tales from its history. The hotel was begun, I said, in 1886, as one of a series of castle-like hotels which the Canadian Railway began to build after laying its railway tracks through the Rocky Mountains. Since Banff was already known as a spa with hot mineral springs, the administration of the railway wanted to build something fancier than they had been planning to build elsewhere and asked Bruce Price, a noted architect, to draft the design. One of the most beautiful sites in Banff was chosen for the hotel: where the Spray flows into the Bow, on a bluff overlooking the two rivers. When William Cornelius Van Horne, president of the Canadian Pacific Railway, visited the construction site, he almost fainted in horror. Someone had been following the blueprints incorrectly and had turned the plans around

180 degrees, so the finest rooms looked out on featureless slopes while the hotel kitchen had a sweeping view of the river valley and mountains. The plans were quickly adjusted, I said, and the hotel opened, in its first iteration, that is, on June 1, 1888, advertised as the largest hotel in the world. With the surge in the number of visitors from Europe and the United States, the hotel grew, so now, I said, there are almost six hundred rooms, though it certainly is not the world's largest. At the turn of the century it had grown in height, I said, so a guest had been quoted as saying that, yes, the new building was, indeed, towering; the only thing that towered higher was the price of drinks at the bar. As I had reckoned, after last night's binge of drinking no one was amused. The hotel acquired its current appearance, what we see today, I said, in the late 1930s, and someone once described it nicely, saying it had "hallways for invalids, towers for stargazers and balconies for lovers." Considering the state we were in, said Daniel Atijas, there was nothing left for us to do but stick to the hallways. Again no one laughed. Its appearance as a castle, which might more readily be described as a paraphrase of castle features, was unconvincing today, and once a French painter who had also been staying at the Banff Centre announced that it was a Hollywood version of a European castle. He said this with disdain, and I had never forgiven him. I could have gone on entertaining them with any number of hotel ghost stories, tales of the celebrities who had stayed there, a story of how the first runway for planes was laid in about 1930, when Benny Goodman decided to visit Banff by plane, but Daniel Atijas was impressed enough with what I had

already related, and this was apparent, so I hurried us through the labyrinthine hotel corridors and down countless stairs, at some points aptly gloomy, until we got to the restaurant, from which stretched a view of the Fairholme Range with its snow-covered peaks. We agreed on green tea at, I confess, my urging, after the waiter reeled off a list of ten varieties, which represented, he remarked, only a small fraction of their supplies in the kitchen. Silence reigned around the table while we were waiting for the tea, as is often the case. Daniel Atijas was absorbed by the view, his lips moving only now and then, as if they were retrieving long-forgotten sentences. Ivan Matulić's grandson sat with his head bowed as if regretting, suddenly, having consented to come with us, though no gesture confirmed this: no twitching of fingers, biting of lips, crossing of legs. He did nothing but be quiet, which is, of course, the most common sign of the worst agitation. I pretended to zero in on reading the menu, peeking furtively over the top and around the edges, though I did find the dessert section absorbing. Had I not been with Daniel Atijas and Ivan Matulić's grandson, that list could have brought tears to my eyes, but as it was, I had to restrain myself, especially because the waiter was already approaching our table with a tray on which he had plates, fragile cups, spoons, a tea pot, a milk pitcher, a sugar bowl, and a bowl of scones. Ivan Matulić's grandson looked up only after the waiter, having served the tea, had moved far enough away, and said it would be best, perhaps, for him to apologize first. Yesterday, he said, at the very beginning he had broached a subject that had been bothering him, but later, he said, as we all knew, that beginning was irreparably damaged, and where there is no beginning, there can be no end. He stopped, looked at us, sipped his tea. He had already spoken, he said, of how he had felt like a prisoner, how he had suffered the pressure of his limited ethnic choices and fled the Croatian language as if it were a ball of fire. Language truly is fire, said Daniel Atijas at that point, except that while some succeed in escaping fire, no one escapes language. Ivan Matulić's grandson said he knew nothing about that; his goal at the time had been to get as far away as possible from his parents' tongue, the umbilical cord that was threatening to kill him, or so he was convinced. As soon as he graduated from secondary school he moved out of his parents' place and rented a house with friends in the older, rundown part of town. To his great surprise, he said, his parents did not protest; they even helped him furnish his room as nicely as possible. His mother, he said, shed a tear or two, but there were no recriminations or quarrels. He was his own man and could do what he wanted with his life. He did not, however, he said, do anything much with it; at first he took every job that was offered, collapsing into bed at night, dead tired, rising the next morning a wretched soul who could hardly wait for each day to pass. Later things got better, he said: he managed to complete a few college courses and focus on accounting, and he got a job in a large petroleum concern, convinced all the while that he was building impenetrable walls around himself with something which, he said, could be described as a sense of Canadian identity. And then, he said, the war broke out in Yugoslavia, and something changed. He began following the news, feeling queasy, recognizing in himself Croatian words that he was convinced he had long since forgotten. He couldn't explain just what had happened, he said, but it was as if he were rid of something, as if he had shed one skin and acquired another, as if he were both forgetting and renewing himself, becoming something he had never been. Even then he had no thought of returning to his family home, but he remembered several old acquaintances, started going to church, frequented two or three cafés; and his world acquired a dimension, which, if someone had asked him earlier, he would have firmly asserted did not exist. Immediately, and he had to say this, he began meeting people who tried to persuade him to go off and fight for Croatia, but though he considered it seriously, particularly while the hostilities were under way against Vukovar and the bombing of Dubrovnik began, he still couldn't see himself in uniform or, even less, wielding a weapon, though those thoughts, slowly but surely, brought him to the idea that he should go to Croatia as a member of a humanitarian organization, as, ultimately, three years later, he did. Now that he was talking about all this so readily, he said, in this old-fashioned hotel with a cup of fine tea before him, how interesting it was that all those years he had never once given a single thought to history. All of it existed for him only in the present, as it was unfolding, and none of it had anything to do with what had gone before, or, at least as far as he was concerned, it was connected only to whatever event had immediately preceded it; in all these years nothing had found its way to him, least of all the articles appearing from time to time in the daily and weekly press that claimed to be espousing an objective, historically founded interpretation of events in Croatia and Yugoslavia. Ivan Matulić's grandson nibbled at his scone and sipped his tea. History had never, he said, meant much to him, for, after all, he had grown up in a time with no history, in a country without a history, on a continent where study was more and more often seen as assembling fragments; there was no interest in the past, only in the present and, possibly, the future, since the past, history, could exist only as continuity, as a totality in which everything, whether a person wanted this or not, was interconnected. For that matter, said Ivan Matulić's grandson, it was not historical quandaries that had prompted him to give up on the idea of going to the Croatian front but that one night in the middle of Calgary he saw a group of young men of Croatian descent beating up two young Serbian men, and while the shouts and groans climbed skyward and blood gushed down shirts and trousers, he hid in the shadow of a garbage container and vomited, holding his own forehead with his left hand the way his mother had held him long ago when he was small. When the sirens of police cars wailed, he fled with the others. Then he understood, he said, that he was not meant for war but for peace, and this momentarily renewed his faith in his shaken sense of belonging to Canada, though soon he lost it again. The passion with which he embarked on exploring his Croatian heritage surprised everyone — himself and his parents included. His father made no secret of his joy when he started taking an interest in the news, asking for explanations, taking an eager part in collecting financial and material support for Croatian refugees, and especially when he asked his father to speak with him every day for at least an hour in Croatian. He felt elated—there was no reason to hide it—at the thought that the thousand-year-old Croatian dream was finally coming true, just as he felt hatred, he said, for all those who stood in the way of that dream. Now he was ashamed of this, but then, he said, then it was a blindness that let him see nothing else. His life became an obsession with the idea that after spending years in the absence of history, he should be where history was happening, even if it wasn't on the front lines, at the very front, but somewhere in the rear, for he knew, he said, that history was written in many places at once, and that each of these was every bit as important, regardless of whether all the events would make it into the history books and regardless of what they would leave out. And so it was, in the fall of 1994, that he found himself in Zagreb. Only two months later, however, frustrated by his desk job and the constant refusal of his superiors to send him into the field, he quit. By then he had contacted relatives in Osijek and Split, and all he wanted, he said, was to be closer to the country and the people who, he was convinced, were making him a happier and better man than he had ever been before. He was not blind, he said, and he wouldn't want us to think he had never noticed certain negative things going on in politics and culture, but he was inclined to embrace the position espoused by one of the Croatian officials when he was still working and taking part in meetings with representatives of the government. When a democracy is young, said the official, the pills are bitter. This was, in fact, said in response to accusations from the opposition that the government had introduced near-blanket censorship. It's not that we control the media, said the official, it's that we will not allow the media to act against the interests of the Croatian state and the Croatian people. And besides, said Ivan Matulić's grandson, all of that didn't interest him much. What did interest him was a bond beyond politics and ideology, a sense of loyalty to the native soil and a sense of the transmission of purity from heart to heart. Like in Zen Buddhism, said Daniel Atijas. Maybe, said Ivan Matulić's grandson, though he knew nothing about Buddhism, and after everything that had happened, he seemed to know nothing about the heart and even less about purity. When on a trajectory of ignorance, a person cannot stop and tends to sink ever deeper until the ignorance reaches the tip of his nose, his eyelids, the crown of the head. And he, he said, discovered that he was mired in muck; he might have been able to speak about it all as an ascendance, a conquest, which acquisition of knowledge really is, but attaining such heights would have been linked to some kind of elation, and for him, he said, there was no such feeling. He reached the heights, one could say, only to sink to the depths. It all began just when he thought he would forge the most powerful bond if he were to learn something about his forebears, and it made sense, did it not? to find out something about his grandfather, the man who predetermined his, this grandson's, fate, having decided to venture off to another continent; one might say instead, he said, that his grandfather had inscribed on the grandson's palm his travel line and his line of return. He showed us his palm and looked at us as if we knew what the lines meant. He hadn't been sure where he should begin, for he had no idea where his family came from, but one evening while out strolling around Zagreb he remembered his grandfather's books and realized that the library was the place to start; there he would finally discover the thread which would guide him through the labyrinth and lead him out. He visited all the Zagreb libraries, and in one of them, perhaps the university library, he wasn't sure, he found two books by Ivan Matulić in the catalogue. Both were travelogues: the first about a summer spent in Iceland, the second about a winter spent on the Norwegian fjords. On the back of the Iceland book he came across the information that the author had traveled several years before over the American continents, that he had traversed them from north to south, or rather, the blurb said, from the Yukon to Tierra del Fuego—travels about which one could read in his books *Among the Mountains and Indians* and *The Pampas Is Burning*. It would be better, he said, not to ask how he finally unearthed the books— the search itself merited a novel—but find them he did, and he learned from the biographical notes that his grandfather was born in 1904 in Osijek, where he mastered the trade of glazier, and from there, having found life's meaning in constant movement, as he said in the foreword to the first book, he set out on his peregrinations. He never said what spurred him to travel, but with the Balkan wars, World War I, the collapse of Austria-Hungary, and the emergence of Yugoslavia in mind, one could see this as a desire for peace and quiet, a flight from the disorder of history into the order of the scheduled arrivals and departures of trains and boats—mimicry of a nostalgic dream of things that never change—or restlessness of the spirit masked by the activity of the flesh. All this was, of course, mere guesswork, said Ivan Matulić's grandson, since his grandfather had died years ago, though he, the grandson, was convinced of the veracity of what he sensed, considering how many times the same pattern had repeated: departure for an exotic, poorly known destination, a stay of several months, acquaintance with local circumstances and beliefs, then a return to Osijek and Croatia, as if these sometimes protracted absences were designed to so whet the returnee's appetite for return that the condition in which he found his country, his home, no longer mattered. That should have told him something, said Ivan Matulić's grandson, but at the time he wasn't yet ready to hear it. Like someone who has discovered the joy of return, even though he had never left, in the literal sense, the place to which he was returning, he believed at first that this was at the heart of what his grandfather had been writing about. Then began, he said, the period of sobering—an apt word, since all love, all elation, is a form of inebriation, and when one is inebriated, as we had all experienced the night before, one's defense mechanisms react more feebly, until finally the person becomes the victim of the drink, or rather the delusion. It is one's own delusion, of course, but delusion is delusion, regardless of its source. In short, his initial indifference toward Croatian political events slowly eroded: ignoring the heightened nationalist rhetoric became harder and harder, as did drawing untenable historical parallels, refusing to take responsibility — all the things which, when he sat down and thought about them, should have bothered him right away. Faced with not being able to understand historical references or allusions that were obvious to everyone he spoke with there, he began, at the same time, to fill in the gaps in his knowledge of Croatian and European history. A young woman named Klara, with whom he shared an apartment, though not a bed, near the train station, advised him not to rush into this; she urged him to give up on what she called his mad rummage backward through the time spiral, especially if he wanted to preserve his pureness of heart, his feelings. But by then it was too late. Once a person ventures into history, he said, extricating himself is not an option. This is what happened. He pulled together what he could find in English, even what he was told had been enemy propaganda; soon his head was spinning with figures, including the data for the living, slaughtered, burned, rebaptized, and disappeared people — in this hellish cosmos, simple disappearance seemed the kindest of fates. The question of where his grandfather was in all of this, he said, insinuated itself wormlike into him, and that worm now squirmed on its way, stopping at nothing and never announcing what it would become in the end. This was the first time he felt frightened, not, of course, in a way that implied terror and quaking; rather, he was filled by what is often called a chilling dread, a fear of the unknown and the amorphous, that swelled inside him and threatened to fill him to the brim. Klara, he said, had been right, but he never liked acquiescing to her, and even if he had, there wasn't

time for it: the purity might at any moment turn into a stain. Perhaps it already had, but he refused to admit this to himself, to
face it, leaving it instead, this stain, somewhere beyond his range
of vision, at the perimeter of his consciousness. In any case, he
said, he gave up on his planned trip to Osijek, using news about
flare-ups of Serbian-Croatian hostilities in eastern Slavonia to
justify not going, though the real reason for his fear was what he
might find in the Osijek libraries and archives. The elation that
had possessed him for several years, that had brought him over-
seas, ebbed, he said, and every morning, while still in the apartment near the train station, he would wake up a slightly different
person, further from what he had been and closer to the man he
had left behind three years ago. He hoped, he said, that we understood him, that we could see how at first he had believed that his
grandfather—when he came to Canada from Croatia—had
scribbled a pledge on the palm of his grandson's hand to go back
there, but then had begun to treat this as a pledge to forget, a call
to embrace the fact that there would always be a place, no matter
where, in which he would never set foot. Since he, the grandson,
had, of course, set foot in Croatia, he said, the pledge no longer
pertained; still, his actions didn't seem irrevocable, and he
thought that if he hastened his return, he might yet be able to
convince himself that nothing had happened, that he hadn't yet
read the writing on his palm. But wouldn't it have been simpler,
Daniel Atijas and I asked, to seek the answer from the very person who knew—from his grandfather? Not anymore, said Ivan
Matulić's grandson, for his grandfather, as he'd said, had died

some years before, at a time when he, the grandson, was not aware of any of these things. Isn't that always the way it turns out? he said. We recall those we need the most when we can no longer reach them. But that is why, after he left Croatia and went back to Calgary, he remembered something else: bags and boxes of his grandfather's things that were in a cupboard in the basement of their house. When his grandfather died, most of his clothing had been given to the Salvation Army, some of his things were thrown away or, like his books, put on a living-room shelf, and everything else, of which there wasn't much—two small bags and three or four cardboard boxes—was piled into the basement cupboard. Ivan Matulić's grandson had no idea, he said, what they held, but when he started opening them, the first thing he found was old pajamas and slippers, then shirts and handkerchiefs, then a warm winter coat that filled a whole box, a toiletry kit including shaving things, two hats, and a plaid scarf, so for the most part he couldn't imagine why these things hadn't been tossed out or given away. At the bottom of a bag he found more copies of his grandfather's books, one of which he gave to the Museum of Natural History and another of which he took to the city library in Calgary. As he was taking them out he touched the hard edge of something with the tips of his fingers, but when he peered into the bag, he couldn't see what it was. He ran his hand along the bottom again and only then realized that something else was in there, but *beneath* the smooth lining. He got a knife from the kitchen, went back down into the basement, and started to cut. In retrospect, he said, as he talked of this and spoke of the knife and the cutting, he could see all the symbolism that went with the words, but as he worked a package wrapped in wax paper out through the slippery incision, he could not have imagined anything of the sort. And was he thinking, asked Daniel Atijas, that the slippery incision was like a vagina and that when he inserted his hand into it, he was much like an obstetrician delivering a new being into the world? Ivan Matulić's grandson answered that nothing like that had occurred to him; at that moment, he had thought of nothing and had been driven by a need to clarify something, learn about himself—that was all. He glanced over at me, but I said nothing. He unpacked the package, he said, and found in it a hardcover notebook, which later turned out to be Ivan Matulić's diary from the first years of World War II, and with it various documents, letters and photographs, a small medal, several banknotes, and a cardboard box like the kind in which ballpoint or fountain pens are sold. Each of these things soon confirmed his fears, he said; the photographs, and letters, and immigrant documents, and parts of the diaries which he managed to read through slowly with the help of a dictionary—all of these things, each in its own way, told him that his grandfather, Ivan Matulić, had fought in Ustasha units during World War II. In and of itself, he said, that information might not be so terrible if one kept in mind the vast number of people who fought on the losing side, but when one learns of the crimes perpetrated against Serbs, Jews, and even Croats, then this was not something a person really wanted to learn about his forebears. He said this as if asking, not stating, so Daniel Atijas and I nodded. In May 1945, as the Communists neared Zagreb, Ivan Matulić's grandson told us, many Croats, especially those who had fought with the Home Guard and the Ustasha forces, left for the Austrian border, hoping they would be able to surrender to the Anglo-American troops there and avoid the doom that awaited them if they fell into the clutches of the Communists. They made it to the Drava River and the border and got as far as the Austrian town of Bleiburg, but there they were tricked by the British army, stripped of their weapons, and returned by train to Yugoslavia, where several tens of thousands of them were massacred and thrown into pits near Kočevje and elsewhere in Slovenia. His grandfather escaped, he said, probably by jumping off the train; after several days of wandering and hiding, he turned himself in to the British, who interned him at a camp for German soldiers. Later, by all accounts, he was transferred to a camp in Italy, and some three or four years after that, he received approval to emigrate thence to Canada, where he went with his son, who later, said Ivan Matulić's grandson, became his father and whom *his* father, the grandson's grandfather, had sent off to northern Italy, probably sensing where things were headed, to stay with his mother's relatives. His father's mother, the grandfather's wife, had died before the war, he said, and she was buried at an Osijek cemetery. The only thing he hadn't told us, said Daniel Atijas, was what was in the fountain-pen box. Ivan Matulić's grandson looked around, then straight ahead, then he twisted sideways, and finally he leaned over the table and the cups of cold tea and said: a human finger. We suddenly found ourselves shrouded in a tent of silence. The commotion, the clatter of dishes, the squeak of rubber soles, all of it could still be heard, but it came to us from farther away, as if someone had moved the entire restaurant out onto the terrace, leaving the three of us in a closed shelter. I remember that I shot a stealthy glance at my own index finger and tried to imagine it severed, separated from the rest, but I could not. I don't know why I looked at my index finger in particular, for Ivan Matulić's grandson hadn't said which finger was in his grandfather's box, but I probably wouldn't have had any better luck imagining any of the others being severed from my hand, arm, body. Had his grandfather, Daniel Atijas wanted to learn from Ivan Matulić, been missing any fingers? No, he had not. If it wasn't his grandfather's, whose was it? He, too, would like to know, said Ivan Matulić's grandson, but he found no hint in the box, or among his grandfather's papers, or in the diary. The only thing he did not try to do was to get in touch with his grandfather's friends, he said, with people who shared his grandfather's convictions, for he couldn't have borne hearing again the story of the thousand-year-old dream, and he doubted, he added, that they knew much more than he did. He chose a different tack. He worked, he said, to reconstruct his grandfather's life carefully, especially the war-time and first postwar years, and in doing so he learned the details he had already mentioned: the escape from near Bleiburg, the time in camps in Austria and Italy, his arrival in Canada in 1948 or 1949, his move to Calgary after six months in Ottawa, his frequent visits to Banff, his life dedicated to the various jobs he held, including excavating dinosaur bones near Dramheller. And then, using the Access to Information Act, the grandson got hold of documents that helped him build a picture of his grandfather's first years in Canada, and that picture, he said, was what completely undid him. As if it weren't enough to face the fact that he was descended from someone who had fought on the wrong side in the war, and who, judging by the severed finger, had done so with relish, he also now had to accept that this same person had worked for a full fifteen years as a spy for the Royal Canadian Mounted Police, responsible for passing on information about the leftists and Communists among the Croats and other immigrants from Yugoslavia. He knew, he said, that there were plenty of people who would have put his grandfather on a pedestal for this postwar activity and who even would have felt that his involvement in containing the spread of evil communism would absolve him of guilt for his part in the Ustasha scourge, but he, the grandson, was unable to think that way; he couldn't and he didn't want to, for evil is evil, and victims are victims, especially when they suffer for ideas, not actions. He would have had a great deal to say on that score, he said as he checked the time, first on his wristwatch and then on the large wall clock, but it was high time he got going, for he still had the drive to Calgary ahead of him and a business dinner that evening, but if we two or just Daniel Atijas were willing, we could get together again tomorrow evening, or better yet, he said, over the weekend. Then he'd have time to finish telling us the story of his grandfather, and we could, he winked, have a repeat performance of some of last night's fun and games. As far as he was concerned, said Daniel Atijas, that suited him fine, but Ivan Matulić's grandson should keep in mind that Daniel Atijas would be traveling on Monday, and though he didn't have a lot with him, he liked having time to pack. At his words, which he tossed off with a cavalier indifference, my heart clenched and I thought it would never release. I thought about them again, the words and the heart, when I got back to the studio. First we said good-bye to Ivan Matulić's grandson and agreed we'd get together again on Saturday afternoon while at the same time declining his offer to give us a ride back to the Banff Centre, mainly because Daniel Atijas said he would enjoy the walk, though only a moment later, as Ivan Matulić's grandson's car was pulling away, he added that we would have to split up because, he said, he still had shopping to do, last-minute shopping; time was zipping by, and since shopping always got on his nerves, he said, it was better if he did it alone, without me, though, he remarked, he would rather be doing it without himself, he had so little patience for shopping, but hey, there was no way around it, especially because he had promised things to many of his friends: books, CDs, tea, nylon stockings, felt-tip pens, exotic spices, and who knows what else, a thousand odds and ends, but even if there had been only one thing to get, he would have felt a special obligation to do so because of the dire situation in his country and because there were many things they couldn't get, and if they were available, they cost more there. In short, once we had crossed the bridge and reached the intersection of Buffalo and the main street, he continued straight while I turned right, deciding, in my despair, to take the long way to the

Banff Centre, as if the length of the route or the magnificent view stretching from the road across the Bow River to the hotel where Ivan Matulić's grandson had just told us his story, or part of his story, as if the length of the path and the surrounding beauty would brighten my mood, my sour mood, caused by those words and the clenching of my heart. Had I run into Mark Robinson or the president of the Banff Centre, for instance, who knows what I would have said, or maybe I would have said nothing, but would have walked by in silence despite their smiles, as if they weren't there and never had been. I met no one, not even tourists; nevertheless, as soon as I reached the Banff Centre area I walked, culprit-like, head bowed. I wanted to get to my studio as fast as possible—that was all I had in mind—and it would be awful, I thought, if something or someone should stand in my way. For the first time I passed by a dozing elk in the woods on the path leading to the studios without a shiver of fear. I never even turned, a little later, when I heard it snort and, most likely, clamber to its feet. I entered my studio and closed the door behind me as if this guaranteed a modicum of safety. None of us can guarantee anything for ourselves, I thought, let alone for others. Everything is self-deception, I thought, every drawing, every hue, every word. I looked into the face that watched me with its many eyes as if it were some sort of rare breed of animal, a newly discovered species, an interloper from outer space, from another planet. Every one of these determinants was true; I should have seen it earlier, understood that what at first looked like an ascension was, in fact, a plummet. I was falling like Icarus, and I didn't know which was more painful: the feathers ripping off, the fall itself, or the hot tar pouring over my flesh, leaving juicy blisters. I tried to calm myself, I tried to reassure myself that everything is an illusion anyway: this used to comfort me, but not now, perhaps because I was among mountains and not on the plains, where everything, even misfortune—and this thought now felt like salvation—would be so different. I said all sorts of things, I know, but I am a painter, not a writer, and I couldn't feel an obligation toward words, at least not my own, though I realized that not a single one of my paintings offered the force of despair that sprang from the words of Ivan Matulić's grandson: there was no comparison. In any case, I was not even working to depict despair in my paintings and drawings. Perhaps I don't really know what it is that I work to depict, but despair has, most certainly, never occurred to me. Again I arranged the face sketches on the table, floor, and chairs, and again I wasn't satisfied. Perhaps I had succeeded in catching the true lines of the face, but I was still far from expressing what I was carrying inside me, from drawing into the face what I felt toward it. I was not sure whether something like that was even possible: to draw yourself onto someone else, into someone else, not as if the face was yours, with your lines, but with your feelings, your inklings, your hopes. This is gibberish, I thought, and gathered up the sheets and put them back into the sketch pad. Just as I was flipping the pad shut and was about to stow it on a shelf, someone knocked. I wanted to rush over, and then I thought to duck behind something, and finally I waited for the knocking to repeat. Up till then

I had managed to evade a visit from Daniel Atijas, having literally dragged him away from my studio on two or three occasions, fearful that if he saw the drawings of the face he might distance himself from me, a little at first, and then further and further, until he had disappeared over the horizon, but now it didn't matter because he was distancing himself anyway; he no longer belonged to me, and no matter what I did, I couldn't alter the slender line of the horizon or his movement, slow but sure, in that direction. At the door, however, when I opened it, Daniel Atijas was not the person standing there, so I needed a few moments to collect myself and exchange his facial features, already drawn in my mind, for the features of the person who was there, Mark Robinson. Troubles never come singly, of course. It was not enough that Daniel Atijas was fading away toward the horizon; now Mark had to be standing in front of me, obstructing my view. I rose up on my tiptoes and peered over his shoulder. There was nothing to be seen, not even an elk on the path. I am on my way out the door, I said to Mark, to check in at the Banff Centre office and see whether the canvas I ordered from Calgary has come, and without waiting for him to say a word I slammed the door of the studio and set out on the path strewn with pine needles. Mark plodded along after me, rumbling about a literary gathering later that evening, at which, or so he'd heard, Daniel Atijas, too, was supposed to be reading. He didn't know what. Nor did I. Had I not already been stung by Daniel Atijas's imminent departure, the fact that he hadn't mentioned the gathering would have pained me even more, so ultimately, in an odd way,

I could be gratified, but I still had to press my left fist to my chest, to the spot under which beat my heart, pounding as it never had before, while behind me, ambling along like a bear, was Mark Robinson, uttering unfamiliar words and meddling with the silence. Isn't that just the way it always is, I thought, that whenever I want to be alone, there is someone standing behind me, even when nobody's there at all. I think it was then, on the path near the little wooden bridge and the musicians' huts, that I first pushed to convince myself to give up, not because of feeling stung or powerless—both things were definitely familiar to me from before, particularly the powerlessness with which I had been living ever since I'd begun painting—but because of feeling tugged by forces that were drawing me into something I had never experienced, a vortex of historical events and interpretations from which, I sensed, I might never wrench free. Living in North America, I thought as I stood in the Centre office with Mark Robinson breathing down my neck, I had begun to believe that history happened to others, that here in Canada we were already living in the future, or at least in a present that had had no past for a very long time. When I later tried to articulate these thoughts—more concisely, of course—to Daniel Atijas before the literary gathering, he made the point that this sense of time was due not merely to geographic coordinates and the specifics of one place or another; there was, he said, a similar readiness to give up on history in all economically advanced countries. History, said Daniel Atijas, is terrible ballast, and those who can, give history a wide berth, which is easiest to do in countries where the

standard of living and ownership allow you a false conviction
that history is over and done with — unnecessary, piddling, super-
fluous, and used up, like old sandpaper. Everything that was
sharp is now blunted, he said, and does nobody any good. And
therein, he went on, lies the greatest rub, for history can never be
completely blunted. Even when it grows dull, it goes right on
slicing and dicing the same as ever, which here, he said, can best
be seen in the example of Quebec, where blunt history, when
needed, can become the most lethal of weapons. This is a paradox worth thinking about, he said, but apparently, he said, as we
waited for the literary gathering to begin, nobody is, just as nobody, he added, seems to be thinking about how history is allowed to exist on this continent in several versions at the same
time, not only in the one penned by the victor but in the version
by the defeated and by the many groups from the social or sexual
or religious margins, and all these histories are embraced as valid,
creating additional turmoil in the mind of every poor soul who,
nevertheless, is prepared — despite being assailed by tales of the
demise of history — to take history as a given, necessary and with
benefits for mental health. I was surprised that he was speaking
of a connection between history and mental health, for based on
things he had said earlier, and especially in the first talk he gave
on June 10, I had had an entirely different impression of his view
of history, and he struck me as the type who does not easily switch
views, especially not ones grounded in personal experience; but
this would not be the first time that mountains swayed a person
so that the person, especially someone from the plains, lost all

sense of direction, both on the outside, their geographic sense, and on the inside, in the sense of heart and mind. But just as I was about to ask him about this, over came the director of the Literary Arts Programs and his wife. It's time, said the director, and we followed him dutifully. First a poet from Chile read, then a playwright from Toronto, then Mark Robinson, and then a poet from Vancouver, a Chinese woman. I could have left at that point, for I found it so tedious listening to all these poems about little moments that meant nothing, probably not even to the poets, not to anybody. After that there was a fifteen-minute break that I spent loudly sipping coffee in a corner of the foyer, though not too loudly, just loudly enough so that Daniel Atijas, standing in the facing corner, surrounded by women, could hear me. A coffee sip, I remember thinking, is like a snake hiss, though I was startled as soon as I thought it by my readiness to liken myself to a viper. I would have loved to hear what Daniel Atijas had to say about that, but the women were tenacious, unrelenting, and only the director of the Literary Arts Programs managed to wrest him free, though Daniel Atijas had to promise he'd be back once the readings were done. Daniel Atijas was first to perform in the second half, and again his voice quavered as he reined in his emotions, though this time he was reading a story instead of an essay on the fate of his country: former country, as Daniel Atijas always added. The story he read—which he announced was brand-new, only recently translated into English—this story spoke of nothing. There was no storyline to it, no events, no central or marginal characters; it seemed to have no beginning or end. It was all

about passage, about language itself—endlessly beautiful and
powerful—and if it sounded this good in translation, I had to
wonder what it had sounded like in the original. I doubt anyone
but I was interested, because when I turned around, I didn't see
a single radiant face, and the president of the Banff Centre did
nothing to stifle his yawns. For me the evening ended when
Daniel Atijas's story came to an end, but I stayed on to hear the
other participants, an essayist from Winnipeg, a novelist from
Mexico, and a poet from Calgary, though I didn't really hear
them, for I was still hearkening, though now only within myself,
to his story's cadence. After lukewarm applause that marked the
end of the reading, the director of the Literary Arts Programs invited everyone to have coffee and dessert and to mingle with the
authors, who, said the director, had shown us once again that
without words there would be no world, or that the world is
words, regardless of the language in which they are spoken or
written. All that was left to ascertain, added the director, was
whether in their world there was room for confections, which, as
everybody knows, are spun not of words but of sugar and choco-
late. He chuckled as if he had said something witty. The people
in the audience stood up, chatter filled the hall, several women,
perhaps the same ones, flocked again to Daniel Atijas, and I tried
to find a spot right behind Mark Robinson, checking out as I did
so the angles with which to gauge the precise angle of my invisi-
bility, and bumped into the poet from Vancouver. A plastic glass
wobbled in her hand, but nothing spilled, and even if it had, said
the poet, she was holding ordinary tap water. She never drank

anything else, least of all carbonated beverages, which are often dyed with chemical substances and can leave nasty stains for which there is almost no remedy, whereas tap water leaves no stains at all, regardless of the kind of fabric. As to the health benefits, she said, that goes without saying. There was nothing further from my mind just then than health. I had always despised the health craze that had been marking, so inappropriately, at least on this continent, the close of the century, a century more diseased than all that had come before it. I put some of the loathing into my painting *Prairie Dream*, in which a capacious old-fashioned bed merges into a prairie landscape. A very fat half-naked man is reclining on the bed. The painting, thanks to the way I shaped the layers of his fat, was meant to be a searing commentary on universal obesity, which I saw as the effect, not the cause, of the health craze, but a critic for the Saskatoon newspaper interpreted the painting as being in praise of obesity, noting that the "volumes of the human body join in their abundance with the erotically shaped forms of the endless prairie, thereby imbuing the abundance with twofold meaning." Nowhere later does he say what that meaning is, thereby adding yet another perplexity to the large number of unknowns in my life. It occurred to me to retell a condensed version of this to the poet, but right then Mark Robinson turned around for whatever reason, which drove me to scooch down closer to the poet, and in doing so, I bumped her arm inadvertently with my shoulder. The plastic cup wobbled again, this time more wildly than before, and several drops splattered her blouse. I began, while still bent over, to apologize, while she, at the same time, protested that I should have no worries, for water, as she'd said before, leaves no stains, but this little fumble of ours drew the attention of Mark Robinson, who swung around in our direction, joined us, and quickly offered his services in wiping the damp spots. Attempting to shield her breasts, the poet also twisted away and crouched, and for a moment the two of us were crouching side by side while above us Mark Robinson brandished a white handkerchief. Then the poet left, Mark tucked his handkerchief back into his pocket, and there was nothing left for me to do but straighten up and face my fate. What was up with me? inquired Mark Robinson. I had suddenly vanished and was nowhere to be found, as if I had dropped into a hole in the ground or, he said, more appropriately for the Rocky Mountains, as if I had soared off into the sky. He knew, he said, that I wasn't painting, because I was never at the studio when he stopped by, and he had stopped by, he said, plenty of times, and he knew something else, he added, but I shouldn't even try to ask him where he'd heard it; he would never say, he said, because when he promised something, he kept his word, and besides, it didn't matter whom he'd gotten it from, but he'd heard that I had gotten myself in trouble or, he said, had found myself out in the open between two historical realities which defied the imagination with their horrors and were threatening to pulverize me. While he was saying this I looked him straight in the eyes and never once blinked. If this is true, said Mark, then it's high time for us to do what we said we'd do and go out and relive the old days. Sometimes, Mark said, reminiscing is the only path to forgetting. Just then the director of the Literary Arts Programs joined us. Readings like the one we have just heard, he said, restore one's faith in the power of words. He looked first at Mark, then at me, but we were silent. Had we seen, he asked, how the faces of the listeners glowed at moments, vivid with having something subtle yet essential pouring into them? As far as he was concerned, said Mark, he was always prepared to pour a little something into himself, and that, he added, always seemed to matter more than pouring anything into anyone else, except, naturally, one particular kind of pouring which two do quite nicely, he said, which he would refrain from mentioning just then. The director of the Literary Arts Programs made a disgusted-looking face and glanced over at me as if expecting my help. I said I wasn't interested in Mark's dodges, I was indifferent to inpourings or outpourings, and I did not agree with the director's observation about the glowing faces, for when, I said, I turned to look around during Daniel Atijas's reading, I did not see a single radiant face; I saw, I remarked, not even a shred of understanding, nary a crumb of readiness to go along with what the story, or, should I say, the absence of a story, was offering. The director of the Literary Arts Programs stared at me, though now with an open abhorrence, which in the corners of his eyes and elsewhere was almost hatred. The story or its absence, who cares? he said, but this reminded him that he had meant to have a word with me about Daniel Atijas. He had been meaning to, he said, for several days now but had never found me in my room or at the studio, and though some things are better done sooner, there are others, like this, he said, which it's never too late to do. He said all this loudly, and though he didn't glance at Mark Robinson, I was convinced that Mark Robinson was privy to everything, and that all this had come from him. Maybe they had used a spare key and searched my studio while I was gone or while I was in my room at night sleeping? I could easily imagine Mark Robinson and the director of the Literary Arts Programs, probably with one or two of the guards from the security service, slinking along the path that led to my studio. I could not recall, however, a single moment when, upon entering the studio, it had occurred to me that something might not have been where I'd left it. For most things I had no special place to stow them; disorder was my order. Only once on the floor under the table had I come across some dark pellets, and alarmed at the thought that they might be mouse droppings, I carefully swept them up, folded them into a newspaper, and tossed them in the trash. Meanwhile, hatred had spread across the face of the director of the Literary Arts Programs, probably stoked by my silence, which he clearly read as a kind of defiance, so I decided to say something. I said I had nothing against us talking about Daniel Atijas, though I did not consider myself to be the best-qualified person as far as he, the director, was concerned. It was possible, said the director of the Literary Arts Programs, that I was not the best qualified, but considering the amount of time I'd been spending with him, I was surely better qualified than most, including him, the director of the Literary Arts Programs, who had seen him, he said, only twice—once at the reception at his house and another time in his office, where Daniel Atijas had spent only fifteen minutes. And besides, said the director, whenever he went looking for him, no one knew where he had gone or when he'd be back, and somebody would say that Daniel Atijas was with me. So, said the director, he wanted to find out what I was up to with the man, where I was taking him, and when I'd be leaving him at least a few minutes free to meet with other people. At some point the hatred had left his face, and his eyes now leered, making me think of a derisive grin. I can't say this did not upset me, this shift from hatred to derision, but even more insulting was the knowledge that Daniel Atijas had never mentioned being at the office of the director of the Literary Arts Programs, if only for fifteen minutes. Instantly, however, I reproached myself for reproaching him, since he never told me things like that anyway. Never, for instance, had he mentioned what he spoke about with one of the Chinese women as they walked around the streets of Banff and then along the river while I followed them from afar, ducking behind a tree from time to time, just as he had never once informed me of a single detail of his personal life, with the exception of the evening when we sat in deck chairs by the pool in which several young women were swimming, whom I used as a segue into a conversation about marriage and women in general. Then, to my great surprise, he said he had been married, but only for three years, and that he had a child, a son, who lived with the boy's mother. That was all. He did not give his son's name, the boy's age, whether he was in school, what color his eyes or hair were, nor did I dare ask, caught short by his sudden candor. When he turned to me and raised his eyebrows in question, I answered that I had not yet met a woman with whom I would be prepared to share all I had, but I still believed that one day I might, that I might at any moment, including right there by the pool, meet someone who could play that role. Daniel Atijas did not respond. Instead, he shrugged and kept his eye on the women in the pool. He did not strike me, I have to say, as the type who was incapable of catching subtle allusions, but everyone makes mistakes, so perhaps I was mistaken in my judgment, though I was more inclined at that point to think of certain life circumstances which can at times have an impact on a person's personality, and there could be no doubt that Daniel Atijas, when in that unfortunate country of his, was living in circumstances that were not likely to arouse anyone's envy. None of that, however, helped me formulate the right response to the words and behavior of the director of the Literary Arts Programs. I had stayed there, standing in front of him like a culprit, lump in my throat, hoping to latch onto some words. Of the triumph that was surely filling Mark Robinson I dared not think, nor could I dwell on the likelihood of this becoming a favorite topic of conversation in the Saskatchewan art circles during the autumn. It would be best, I told the director and Mark, for me to bring Daniel Atijas himself over, and they could ask him directly whatever they wanted to know. Without waiting for their response, I stepped boldly over to where Daniel Atijas was still standing amid the bevy of women. When I got there I turned, before saying anything, and looked back at Mark Robinson and the director of the Literary Arts Programs, but they were gone from sight. Daniel Atijas smiled at me and raised his glass in greeting as one of the women launched into her impressions of the latest Woody Allen movie, particularly the music, which she had been coming back to ever since she saw the film and could not forget no matter how hard she tried. I didn't know how to respond, but she wasn't waiting for a response; she went right on retelling scenes and interpreting, as she said, the remarkable examples of ingenuity on the part of the director, editor, and cameraman. While I nodded politely, I fidgeted and shot glances in all directions until I glimpsed Mark Robinson by the hall entrance. I couldn't see the director of the Literary Arts Programs, but if Mark was looking to get out of there, the director wasn't far behind. I tried to draw Daniel Atijas's attention, and when I failed, I inserted myself, not without a jostle, between him and a woman who was picking crumbs and lint off his shirt. I don't know exactly why, just as I didn't know what I'd say to him, and I knew even less why the words of the director of the Literary Arts Programs had so upset me, but while Daniel Atijas went right on conversing over my shoulder I hissed that this was the last minute, that we must leave at once, and I was already dragging him toward the entrance through which the sizeable frame of Mark Robinson was just then ambling. It would have been easier, however, to push our way through brambles than through a cluster of art and literature lovers. Every two or three steps we were forced to halt, not because of me, of course, but because of Daniel Atijas, who was asked questions, asked to shake hands and smile, and even asked to sign copies of his books in English, and when we finally made it to the door, Mark Robinson was no longer anywhere to be seen. If such a big man could disappear so readily, I knew we had no hope of finding the director of the Literary Arts Programs. Daniel Atijas threatened not to take a single step farther until I explained what was going on, but instead of offering a real explanation, I mumbled something about there having been a misunderstanding and asked if he'd join me for a walk. At first indecisive, he did agree, but while we were walking among the buildings of the Banff Centre he insisted—my efforts to divert the conversation to other subjects notwithstanding, to the art of preparing sushi, for instance—that I explain my, at the very least, unusual behavior, and having no way around it yet also quaking at the thought of him flying into a rage and leaving me in the lurch out there in the dark, I explained that this behavior of mine, which was out of line, no argument there, came from the realization, which hit me during the reception, that he had enemies at the Centre. By the way, lest I forget, that evening we did not encounter a single elk, and that fact persuaded me to promise myself that at the first available opportunity I would pay more attention to the habits of elks, for each time I noticed their absence, I'd wonder where they had all gone and how it was that they all knew they didn't have to be standing where they otherwise stood every day and night. Daniel Atijas laughed, not at the elks, since I hadn't mentioned them, but at my claim that he had enemies at the Centre. I told him this shouldn't worry him, because it was mostly a consequence of something typical of prairie dwellers—not all of them, of course, I said, but a number—

especially those who were right-wing in their political thinking or bent. Somewhere, I told him, I had read that the prairie populist movements were rooted in the rich soil of intolerance that had produced a dualistic view of the world, and this dualism produced, I said, a simplistic divide of people into friends and foes, and everyone who was not a friend, or whom you didn't understand, or whose customs were strange to you, everyone like that could be only a foe. Daniel Atijas laughed again, adding that he had never bought into generalizations like these, and now, after all that had happened in his former country, he believed them even less, particularly because, as nearly everyone claimed, the country had come apart at the seams and the war had erupted because of similar hostile feelings from times gone by or perhaps, as some claimed, he said, because hostile feelings were always there in the genes, mind, heart, and guts of every person who lived there. Because of that, he said, he had made an effort to pin down the crux and thrust of the hostility and knew, he said, of no better explanation than one in the wisdom of the Talmud: if two people come to us for help and one is a foe, help the foe first. This, of course, he added, had to do with the wise Talmudic saying that a true hero is a person who turns enemies into friends and also with the biblical admonition that one should not harm foreigners. Those, like the Jews in Egypt, who have felt on their own hide what it means to be an outsider, are especially enjoined not to do that, though folk wisdom has reduced this to a much more practical measure; hence among Yiddish sayings there is one asserting that a friend costs nothing while a foe you pay for, so, he said, it follows that making friends is better and costs less and that he who is a foe to himself will have the most enemies. I told him I understood what he was saying and that I could respond with the words of Paul Muni, who said something along the lines of, if you ain't got enemies, you ain't got nothing, but that my intention, my response, was merely coming from my concern, really my fear, that he might be needlessly hurt. In saying so, I added, I understood full well that a person, whether he wanted to or not, had made habitual the idea of enemies and that I would not be off base if I were to say that having enemies spurred one on more than having friends did; in my thoughts I gave more time to my real enemies than to my true friends. What I still didn't understand, I said, or what I was not prepared to accept, had *never* accepted, was the notion that human society could prevail *only* by basing its development on hostile feelings, hatred, rupture, and division. No one could convince me of that, I said, attempting to send him a knowing look just as we were standing under a street lamp. I doubt he noticed, even though I was twisting my neck around and even leaning into it a little; just then he was staring up at the sky, his head lifted, as if summoning witnesses. He was of the opinion, he said, that the two of us were speaking of more or less the same thing, though perhaps in different words. He, too, he said, was convinced that enmity was not an inevitability for humankind but was learned, which would mean, he said, that this was one more of the things bound to the evolution of human consciousness, to the elevating of mankind above unconscious nature, and that it represented a part of the price a person paid. We are created to be worse so we can be better. But if this is the price of improvement, I said, then I do not intend to pay it, even if I ultimately end up without friends or enemies. Daniel Atijas disagreed. No matter what he thought of the war in Yugoslavia, he said, though he had trouble with the prevailing opinions about inbred hatred, he had to admit that the presence of an enemy created a certain vital, even intellectual dynamic that could never be sparked merely by the company of friends. It might be, he said, that the prairie provinces were advancing precisely because their mechanism for finding enemies was prompting a constant closing of the ranks, and such a cohesion, he said, would probably not be possible without that duality, not possible in a world in which there were only friends. After all, he said, though he didn't know where he'd come across this, it is easier and more reliable to believe foe than friend, and the thinker, whose name he couldn't recall, was right when he said that one should be more careful in choosing one's enemies than one's friends. At that point we were on the road that ran down to the visitors' parking lot and the exit from the Centre, and I suggested we go back, but he was prepared, he said, to go all the way to the place where the road curves and there's the view of the grand old hotel and the Bow River, and he would be glad if I would go with him, especially as I hadn't yet informed him, he said, of who this enemy was that he had acquired at the Centre, whether he meant to or not, now that his departure was steadily approaching; this enemy, or enemies, who could say, could not now play such an inspirational role as he, or they, would have played had he met him, or them, on his first day in Banff. He did hope, he added, that it wasn't Ivan Matulić's grandson, because for reasons that he would rather not go into just now, he said, that would have really saddened him and marred the beauty of his stay at the Banff Centre. I hastened to reassure him, preferring not to go back to the grandson's story, but it was too late. I felt a warm tremor in his voice and sensed a vigor in his steps, and probably, had there been more light, I would have seen a glimmer in his eyes; and while we stood there and watched the lavishly lit hotel, I mindfully erased the grandson's features within myself until there was nothing of him left. It seemed as if Daniel Atijas, having listened to my dissuasions, had lost interest in the identity of his enemy; a full fifteen minutes passed during which he said not a word, but when we turned and started back up to the Centre, he explained that the encounter with Ivan Matulić's grandson stirred in him a long-since-extinguished faith that there was a chance, in the region of his former country, to re-kindle the trust which, he would have said if anyone asked, had been lost forever. It's a bit of a paradox, he said, that he con-cluded this after encountering a person who was not from there, but sometimes one must start from a distance to come to the heart of light, or heart of darkness, either one. This did not mean, he said, that he was not interested in who his enemy was at the Centre, but what mattered to him more now was mending bridges that, he had thought, were burned forever, and he was convinced, he said, that I would understand with my whole heart and approve. Of course, I said, though I was grateful for the darkness, because I always blush when I lie. What Ivan Matulić's grandson has shown me, said Daniel Atijas, is especially precious as a confirmation that there can be no remorse until one admits to one's own guilt, a stark contrast to the demands being heard from all over his former country, that there can be no repentance of one side until the other, or a third party, or however many, confess to their culpability. And in the process, he said, there was no talk of one's own guilt or responsibility, because the premise was the certainty, he said, that there was no guilt at all to be borne by whichever party was speaking. So, he said, where he came from, in his former country, it turned out that no one, in their own eyes, bore any blame; Sartre had put it that hell is always other people. Ivan Matulić's grandson, he said, was the first person who, one way or another, had offered something different, meaning that he had shown the readiness—when he said "hell"—to point to himself. And that, Daniel Atijas went on, was from a person who was not directly involved, though, he said, one could say that in a special way, no matter how many generations a person is away from his ancestral turf, his membership there can never be lost. You can go away, he said, you can live on a different continent, you can plow another field, but you will never get that first dirt out from under your fingernails, that fertile black loam that always, no matter what, marks your only true home. Most important, he said, and it happened after he had heard the grandson's story, was a resurgence of his will to go back to his country, what was left of it, led by a new hope, or anticipation of hope, in contrast to his feeling when he arrived in Banff, when he first appreciated the serenity of these mountains and when he thought there was nothing that could budge him from the spot, that here he would stay forever even if it meant living in the woods or under a bridge, because he was so sickened by everything he had left behind, which he was seeing, as never before, in such a harsh light that it was painful. Incredible, he said, how a person gets used to altered living conditions, how much he himself had been prepared to give up on everything, including morals and shame, only to stay alive as long as possible. Survivors, those of concentration camps in World War II, have written about that eloquently, he said, particularly Primo Levi, though Levi's suicide, he said, does bring into question the likelihood of healing completely after such an experience confirms that sometimes life is only a mask hiding a death that actually happened long ago. He would not want, he said, for me to think he was comparing his lot to the hideous fate of those who bore the brunt of Nazi ideology, but the drop in the standard of living and values in his country, also the result of ideology and obviously lower on the pain scale, had an equal impact on the scale of genuine psychological horror, for life crumbled irreversibly in both cases, and irreversibility is what mattered. But, he said, that was not what he had meant to talk about. Responsibility for one's choice, for the decision to stay in his country, no matter how it turned out, was something he could not shrug off on anyone else; it had to be his responsibility, and he would not be shouting his pain from the rooftops or, like many of the artists of his former country, hawking it to an assortment of world artistic and other foundations, which, by supplying funding, were washing clean—and he believed this deeply—public opinion in their countries and contributing in practical ways to concealing the truth about what they, with their political and economic decisions, had really done to the countries that had been vilified, such as his. He was not sure, he said, whether I would be able to understand all of this, a tangled morass, and also the subtle play of daily and global politics as well as the manipulation of the media, for all this, one way or another, was interrelated and had contributed to his belief that nothing better than his meeting with Ivan Matulić's grandson could have happened. It was good that we were already near the Art Centre at that point, for had we been further down the road or in the woods, I probably would not have been able to resist walking away. I would have spun around on my heel and left him in the dark. As it was, we were so close to the reception desk that I bit my lips and held my silence until we neared Lloyd Hall, where our rooms were. American society, Daniel Atijas then said, as if this was what he had been thinking about the whole time, is founded on respect for the individual, while European societies are founded on respect for the collective. To rise up in the name of America, he said, means to champion individuality, while to rise up in the name of any European country means to champion the right to be a part of the collective. At first glance, he said, this had nothing to do with what we were talking about, but he was sure that in this rift, which, by the way, was growing larger by the day, hid one of the key assumptions needed for understanding the current world order. Could it be, I asked, that he had not seen the paradox of such a statement, for it was precisely the European states, almost without exception as far as I could tell, who had denied this right to his country? I am not sure he answered. He may have only shrugged and left. I was suddenly standing there alone right when nothing was further from my mind than solitude. Doubled over on the floor of my studio this night, I thought for the first time that I should burn all the drawings of the face that I had made, and had I been anywhere but Banff National Park, where they would have arrested me for a candle flame lit on a forest meadow, let alone for a blazing pyre of failed stabs at art, I would probably have nothing left at this point but a box full of ash, the fitting end to every cremation. Instead of burning them, I gathered them together and began to draw again, but I gave myself over fully to the details, such as the left corner of the lips and the tiny web of wrinkles along the edge of the eyelids. Then I dropped off to sleep. When I awoke, I saw a bird on the branch of a conifer. I didn't know what that meant, nor whether birds have any special meaning at moments when dreams dissolve into waking, just as I didn't know whether the number eight, the number of my studio, meant anything besides being a number, and all this, all this quest for meaning, was a sign of my agitation, my effort to find comfort or at least relief by searching for the special meaning in particular things or events to resist the pressure of anticipating the inevitable fear of departure. Not mine, of course, not mine. I lay on my back, listened to the morning sounds of the mountains and woods, and thought about a new beginning. Thinking about a new beginning is a fine defense mechanism, especially at moments when nothing can change whatever it was that came before the new beginning. This doesn't change anything, I knew, but sometimes it does a person good to breathe in deeply without effort and slowly release the breath at will, exactly the way one wants to. Our life, I said over breakfast to the playwright from Toronto, is like a sack of potatoes: if we want to keep them, we must constantly pick through them and snap off the sprouts. The playwright asked if might he jot that down, because it was, he added, an excellent line for the very scene he was working on, in which the protagonist decides to leave her husband and start over. I have never liked the potato, said the playwright, and mashed potatoes made him gag, but there you have it, sometimes we are most helped by things we like least; he might just start eating potatoes, who knows, out of a sense of gratitude for the inspired resolution to a scene that had stymied him. I didn't mind us sharing the potato inspiration, I told him, but while he was talking I was darting glances every which way. It seemed odd that Daniel Atijas hadn't come down to breakfast, and I could imagine any number of reasons to explain this, the worst being a tryst with Ivan Matulić's grandson. The playwright did not stop retelling his scenes, in which more and more places cropped up where the potato signaled salvation, meanwhile continuously shoveling milk-soaked oatmeal into his mouth, so that several times after he sputtered his words I had to pick the moist specks off my forehead and cheeks. Then several more people joined our round table, so the playwright forgot the potato or maybe found another source of inspiration for his limping scenes. I knew none of the new arrivals, though two of the young women, with long faces and hair done up trimly in pony-tails, clearly ballerinas, shot me glances in which there was a trace of recognition. If I did know them, I couldn't remember, and had I tried, I wouldn't have been able to, as all my thoughts were tied up with worry about Daniel Atijas's absence. I may be exaggerating when I say it was worry, because what filled my thoughts was more like anger than anxiety, and I was feeling be-trayed rather than curious about his whereabouts. I remembered how one day soon after he arrived, at a moment when I was trail-ing around after him through the Centre and Banff, I noticed how his hair was growing in a tangle down his neck, reaching all the way to the edge of his shirt collar, where it disappeared and probably joined up with the hairs that covered the upper part of his back and shoulders. Had I had a comb just then, I don't doubt that I would have smoothed those locks; had we known each other better, who knows, I might have taken him to a hair stylist. A haircut in Banff, I would have told him, is a novel experience, for a person, so high in the mountains and freed of the ballast of needless hair, feels he might soar. Nothing holds you back as much as unruly hair, lifeless locks, and split ends. As someone who grew up in the sixties, I probably shouldn't be saying this, but it is difficult to resist change in a society in which a constant state of flux is the sole condition that merits attention — other people's attention, of course, because other people's attention, in this society, is all: nothing else matters. Whatever else does not attract enough attention is condemned to oblivion, to sinking like a stone. I thought about that while I stared at the back of Daniel's head and neck on the streets of Banff, and I thought of it again the other evening while I focused on drawing details; I even tried to summon the scene, the tangled hair, some of which was pure white. Those hairs so entranced me that several times I drew the place where his eyebrows knit, trying to catch the play of light and shadow, the tiny wrinkles above the bridge of his nose, and a droplet of sweat that happened to show up like an interloper. I suddenly wanted to drop my head to the table right next to the bowl of oatmeal and fall asleep among all those simultaneous voices and stay that way, secure in my desolation, until Daniel Atijas came along and woke me up. Instead I got up, raised my hand in a gesture of farewell, as if I were an Indian chief, and turned, ready to go. I turned slowly, as if I would never make it around to face in the opposite direction. I turned again on the stairs when I heard Mark Robinson's voice, but this time faster, as if speed could help. What is so absurd here, I had said to Daniel Atijas when we had our first long, serious conversation, is that artists come to the Centre seeking solitude, dedication to their inspiration and their work, but most often they cannot for the life of them elude the curiosity and envy of those who do not succeed in finding either. It's easiest here, I said to him, to do nothing, and that is exactly what most of them do, pretending all the while, of course, that they are working on something great or at least that they never stop thinking about their work. This notion, I said, that artists should isolate themselves from others, from society, which should be the source of their work — this idea is misguided and so absurd in a system that has long since ceased endorsing isolation for any one of its segments. The notion smells of segregation, isolation, classification by any other determinant except general membership in the human race, which is forbidden and politically out of sync today, but artists continue to be set apart in reservations; this one here happens to be situated in the middle of a national park traversed every year, I said, by three to four million tourists, and we are expected to create works amid all the frenzy, works that express our serenity and focus on questions of form and content, the resolution of the dilemmas of poetics. I don't know why I spoke so furiously at the time, just as I don't know how all of this relates to the tangle of hairs on Daniel Atijas's neck, but when I next had a chance to see the nape of his neck, it was freshly barbered. I don't know who had taken him to the hair stylist; maybe he went on his own—after all, he struck me as the type who figures out how to find his way around an unknown city with ease, and Banff, hand on heart, is not an overly challenging urban labyrinth—but it is quite certain that Daniel Atijas did not then look like the kind who was ready at any moment to soar into the air. That's how it is with some people: the more you free them of the ballast that is holding them down, the heavier they get. Instead of rising, they sink; instead of growing, they shrink. I may be overstating this: perhaps the snipping of a little hair from the neck and behind the ears cannot be fairly compared to other feelings of liberation and levitation, especially not to those which spring from a long-lasting reliance on certain psychophysical skills, but I feel this way every time I step out of a hair stylist's. A person who has just had a haircut and doesn't smile when he looks at himself in the mirror while the stylist brushes the hair off his shoulders, that person has something terribly wrong with him that may eat him alive. When I saw the freshly trimmed hairs on Daniel Atijas's neck, I wondered whether he smiled after getting the haircut, and I have to admit that I was at a loss for the answer. I didn't have it then, nor did I have it later, nor while I did what I could to untangle them while drawing the detail of his tangled hairs, or as I did—while standing at the entrance to the dining hall—what I could, though feebly, to untangle the morning, a morning that was slowly but surely, whether I liked it or not, turning into day. All in all, I didn't have much time—perhaps, who knows, I never did—but if I wanted to get something done, there was no time for waffling. I am forever surprised by the fact that time passes more speedily between mountains than it does out on the prairie, though never, when speaking of time, should one talk of facts, for time does not exist, so it cannot be measured the same way phenomena and things can be that are, or at least seem to be, real. Whatever the case, there were still two or three days before the moment of Daniel Atijas's departure, and they seemed, regardless of length, inadequate for all I had in mind, especially for finishing the picture of the face, and this was not only because of my working slowly but also because of the feelings that kept rising up and becoming impassable obstacles. The faster time passed, the slower I worked. I made no effort to explain this to Daniel Atijas, especially after his assertion, repeated several times in various circumstances, that time in his country had stood still. When he first said this, I had thought he was still speaking of the plain, of that sense of its endless expanse and the drop beyond the horizon when a person really has the impression that time, mid-plain, stands still, but he had something different in mind and was thinking, he said, of time as a reflection of life, and in his country, time, he said, became a quagmire, a temporal rotten egg, and as with all rotten eggs, nothing could come of it, nothing but foul smell. Time that reeks, said Daniel Atijas, has never been recorded as such. I tried to imagine life in a place like that but couldn't. The only thing I did say was that this must be what one of the circles of hell was like, at which Daniel Atijas laughed and said that in comparison to the stench in his country the stench of hell was, to his nostrils, a breath of fresh air. And he had lovely, slim nostrils, which quivered a little whenever he was excited or raised his voice. I attempted in one of the drawings to record that quiver, sketching the outlines using a similarly shaky hand, but that didn't do it. Many more static attempts also didn't work — when, for instance, I sought the shadow cast across his cheek under his jutting cheekbone. I don't know how I could ever have believed in the possibility of capturing, in an artistic rendering, one quivering nostril, or even both, either way. Our capacity for self-deception is incredible, I thought, and I trust that Daniel Atijas would have agreed if only he had shown up and given me the chance to ask. Instead of him, on the steps appeared Mark Robinson; he had finally caught up with his voice, the voice I had heard as I was leaving the dining room. He grinned as if nothing had happened the evening before. Then he thumped me on the back and invited me that evening, if my obligations allowed, to get together with him and finally spend some time with our memories. Memories, said Mark Robinson, are the single constant in this changing world. I know, I said, and I really did know, because that was a line from one of his popular poems, so popular that children read it in the Saskatchewan elementary schools. I promised I would give it a thought, but I didn't dare promise anything more than that, though I feared that the morning might never end, that the previous evening was something only archaeologists still cared to seek, and that sooner or later I would sniff the reek of stagnant time, the same stink Daniel Atijas had been talking about. When that happens, I thought, even the mountain peaks won't help, and it won't matter whether a person is in the middle of the plain or at the highest point above a vertical cliff. And besides, one falls into, not out of, oneself, right? Maybe I shouldn't be speaking of falling just now, but some things do surface with no intention on our part, no matter what the psychiatrists claim. To say that everything is linked, that a pear dropping from a tree somewhere in the heart of Europe has anything to do with a horseshoe that flies off the hoof of a horse in southern Alberta and kills a boy perched on a fence, to claim that between these events and hundreds, thousands, millions of others there is some kind of cause-effect link, not obvious yet incontrovertible, is the pointless effort of a superior human mind that does not grasp its humble scope. I didn't say this to Mark Robinson, because I didn't want to talk with him, and while he was walking away I quaked at the possibility of his suddenly turning around and coming back, but as soon as he'd crossed the path and headed toward the building with the swimming pool and sports hall, I thought of the pear snapping off the branch and that hurtling horseshoe. They were, they should be, my bulwark against the onslaught of those who work to persuade us that our behavior is nothing more than a repeat of pre-set patterns and that, no matter what we think, we are merely entering data into a fixed equation of vital and spiritual structures of whatever, according to these interpretations, makes us all the same. Identical, I should say. Anyway, when I thought at that moment of a cliff and of falling, I wasn't thinking of a real cliff and a real fall; if I had anything in mind at all I was envisioning a sort of fresco or painting of a person's free-fall, his plummet from celestial heights. I was thinking, in short, of how one falls through space while actually sinking into oneself, into what used to be called the human soul. And as I walked away from the dining hall, taking the path that ran by the cemetery, I said to myself that I really ought to ask Daniel Atijas whether he had noticed how people no longer refer to the human soul as they used to, as if everyone has figured out what it really is or, more likely, as if, today, no one cares any longer about looking into the human soul, more than anywhere else, for answers to the essential questions of our existence. Why ask questions, the heralds of our time might say, when we are pleased with how we live? Dissatisfaction spawns doubt, doubt spurs questions, questions are a reflection of our insecurity, our insecurity gives rise to a feeling of inequality, inequality provokes envy, envy is another name for evil. None of that, they say, exists today. No one even tries to ask the question of the meaning of life, because practical science, fed by a groundswell in the economy, has begun to negate the need for a philosophical framing for life's meaning; it offers the possibility of genetic predetermination, modification of mental and emotional determinants, and an endless prolonging of life. To wonder about life's meaning, to tremble over the fullness of experience, to think of happiness, to doubt—all this begins to seem like ballast dragging us downward and threatening to sink us. Death is, simply put, no longer in fashion. Cemeteries, I thought as I neared the cemetery wall, will be unnecessary, and trades such as the art of digging graves or carving names into marble tombstones will vanish, as has happened with scribes or will happen soon with people who repair typewriters. We will all be alive, and we will live forever, or rather they will—they, not we, or at least not I, because I will not have the good fortune, or, I'd rather think, misfortune, to live long enough to greet the triumph of genetic manipulation. I couldn't explain to myself where all these thoughts of death come from unless they have something to do with Daniel Atijas's imminent departure. Every departure is, after all, a little death, as an Arabic poet, if I am not mistaken, once wrote, and the proximity of the cemetery, the almost-tangible weight of the uncountable deaths, surely must have influenced the flow and substance of my thoughts, even though I saw a young man and woman kissing by the cemetery gates. The kiss meant nothing to me, nor did the man's hand, thrust deep into her pants, and even if their embrace did touch me a little then, it also darkened my sour spirits, casting a gloom I hadn't felt since arriving in Banff, which only worsened once I came out onto the main street and mingled with the bustling throng of tourists; it made my face, as I saw in the glass of a shop window, into a scowling mask. No one, true, turned to look after me, but that was because the passersby, upon seeing my black expression, thought it wise not to test their luck and turn around. If his face looks like that, I imagined them thinking, what might the back of his head look like? Those who did spot me—and what with the crowds they could only have seen me while walking past—would instantly hush all conversation, and having passed me by, would walk on in silence. Just as an icebreaker smashes through ice, so I plowed through all that human cheer. For hours that day I paced the streets of Banff, feeling the whole time as if I were marching over the pages of an album of the animal kingdom. From Fox Street I crossed to Badger; from Otter onto Wolf; Bear took me to Buffalo; Grizzly ran parallel to Otter; Rabbit merged with Moose; Caribou came out to the river. Had someone seen my peregrinations from above, who knows what sort of contours they would have discerned, etched by my movement into the pavements of the town. I went to the riverbank, sat on a bench, smelled the water. Now, I thought, when no one can see my face, we can all breathe a sigh of relief. I bent over, ran my hand through the rippling river surface, winced at the cold. I raised my fist and watched as all the water poured out of it between my fingers, first in little jets and then drip by drip. Once it was all gone,

I wiped my hand on my pant leg. I walked along the river, tripping here and there, as if my feet betrayed me. I came to a bend and saw a bridge. On the grass parkway reaching all the way to the Banff Park Museum, nearly surrounded by crowds of delighted tourists, two elks were grazing. From time to time, they lifted their heads and registered with indifference the clicking of cameras and glaring of flashes. I turned left toward the post office and stepped in bird droppings. My left leg slipped. I stumbled, lost my balance, and caught myself on my right hand and right knee. When I straightened up, there was a green stain. Ah, I thought, now that would be something useful that a good natural history museum could do: provide information on how to get chlorophyll stains out of various kinds of fabric, especially linen, instead of collecting wild animals that have been hunted and shot and the signatures of feckless vagabonds. I was so furious that I could have gone straight into the museum and up to the second floor, smashed the glass of the display case, and ripped out the page with the ornate letters which, lined one up next to the other, spelled the name of Ivan Matulić. A horrible day, I thought while I stood at the congested intersection across from the bank and waited for the light to change. A day stripped of substance, I thought, as I crossed over to the other side of the street: a day with no properties, a day of endings, of defeats. I set out along Buffalo, resolved to take the long way back up the mountain all the way to the Art Centre, but suddenly I felt I wouldn't be able to. I was sinking; my heart flagged, deflated like a punctured ball, and I probably would have collapsed into the ditch had a gunmetal-gray jeep not pulled over beside me and honked. The darkened glass window lowered soundlessly, and I saw the director of the Literary Arts Programs inside. Perhaps it would have been better had I slid into the ditch and avoided catching his eye, I thought, but now it was too late, the director of the Literary Arts Programs smiled, beckoned for me to get into a car so capacious that Mark Robinson might have been lurking in there somewhere, which as a possibility at any other time would have been enough to dissuade me from gripping the handle and opening the car door, let alone settling into the leather seat, but my knees were buckling, my mouth was dry, the soles of my feet stung, my thighs were cramping, so with an effort I finally clambered in, as if, I confess, when lifting myself, I were lifting a crate of lead. I think I fell asleep that instant. I must have, for when I opened my eyes again we were parked by the reception building. I couldn't see the director of the Literary Arts Programs anywhere. The digital clock on the instrument panel indicated that lunchtime was over, though, I thought, no one would say a word if I were to go in, pick up a tray, and serve myself a bowl of soup. There was always leftover soup, I thought, though they'd use up the cold cuts and the steamed vegetables. Nor was there ever, I thought, enough ice cream, though there was always all the pudding you could ask for, and pudding is nicer anyway. I didn't want any. I got out of the jeep and, going down the slope, made my way slowly toward the studios. I walked gingerly over the pine needles and dry grass, going from one pine tree to the next as if I feared someone might see me. No one could have, I was certain, but at once I remembered that too great a sense of certainty paves the way for a lasting uncertainty, which I had read in an old anthology of practical advice for success in life, and, sure enough, when I looked up, there was a magpie on a tree branch. Somewhere farther off a door slammed. In the woods, with or without magpies, no one expects to hear a door slam, and it so alarmed me, it was so startling, so much at odds with the surroundings, that for the next few minutes while my heart pounded I was prepared, if need be, to turn and run away at a sprint. A minute later, once I'd come up to the path near the studio fashioned from a fishing boat, I saw that what had slammed was a shutter, which, slapped by wind or a cross draft, was knocking between the wall and the window frame, and this was obviously not the first time, for on the wall where the shutter had banged was a broad swath of scraped wood, pale on the uneven background. I would have liked to show this to Daniel Atijas, to draw his attention to how the pain of the wood was light in color, unlike the pain we feel, which is always dark, often black. In our culture, I wanted to say, pain is never depicted as light except in cases when the pain is seen as a doorway opening to something higher, usually divine. In all other cases, I would have told him, pain opens toward the dark, or, more precisely, pain shuts in with darkness, and from that pain, one is blinded, even when the pain, as with powerful migraines, has to do with light, an abundance of glare, a feeling that the world around the person in pain is turning into tresses of radiance. The eyes are open wide, but the gaze goes nowhere. Looking without seeing, as when staring into darkness. Just then, thinking there might be no difference at all between light and dark, I tripped over a tree root, one of the many intersecting the forest path, lurched, staggered, but still held my balance. When I straightened up again, I saw Daniel Atijas. He was sitting on the steps to my studio—on the top step, to be precise—reading. I don't know what the book was, I never asked, but it entranced him completely, because though my staggering must have disturbed the serenity of the woods, he was glued to the open page, showing in no way that he was aware of my presence. Every painter dreams of a moment when he can dedicate his full attention to a subject who is totally free of any awareness of that attention, but I had no benefit from the moment. I had no paper or pencil, no canvas or brush; only for a moment did it occur to me to slip into the bushes and continue watching him unobserved, and then, as if he sensed my quandary, Daniel Atijas licked his finger, turned the page, and looked up, and I coughed right then the way a person does who has just reached the end of a trying journey. Daniel Atijas's whole face was open to me, and more than ever before he looked like a boy. If I hadn't stopped myself right then, I wouldn't have stopped even once I was between his widespread thighs. This I know. He had started by worrying why I wasn't there, said Daniel Atijas, which did not mean that he had stopped worrying; in fact, he would be worrying still had he not had a book in his pocket, which he had begun, fitfully, to read, he said, as if he had never before in his life read a book, and soon the events in the book so engrossed him that every worry fell away, and the only thing he wanted to find out was what would happen next, which would have been a simple matter had he not started reading the book from the middle, so he kept having to flip back to figure out why some of the characters were saying or doing things, and this became more and more complicated as he leafed back and forth — a movement between past and future, which is, in essence, he said, like real life, what life really is, just as he had said before to Ivan Matulić's grandson. In the end he had begun to think that all books should be written that way or at least published that way, with the pages displaced, which would turn reading into the constant search that is, in his profound belief, he said, the very essence of reading, though that doesn't matter so much; more important is that all this contributed to the absence of all worry, and now, when I had finally turned up, he said, it was clear just how much this, his reading, had been the right choice. Now, he said, he could put the book back into his pocket, and into his pocket it disappeared. If we were in Saskatchewan, I thought, none of this could happen. I still didn't dare move. On the plains, I thought, every movement is a form of standing still, while in the mountains you are always active, at some stage of moving, forced to climb or slow your descent. What goes on in the plains only happens through conscious effort, while in the mountains, it happens by itself. When I stand here, I thought, I am actually walking, or falling, which may be the same thing. Of course, had I really been walking, I would already have been between Daniel Atijas's widespread legs, and I was not there — that at least I know. But still he had thought of something at one point, Daniel Atijas went on, patting his pocket gently as if to console the book that had suddenly dropped into darkness; he had recalled why he had come looking for me at the studio and resolved to wait, no matter how long it took. Now this, no doubt about it, was passion — albeit unexpected — for though I knew that under his serene demeanor Daniel Atijas possessed a fervid spirit, I had not believed he would be able to show it. I wasn't sure whether to be glad or worried: glad that I still, at least like this, could stir someone's passion, or worried that my judgment — which I prided myself on, and not without reason — had lost its edge. All of a sudden it hit him that afternoon, continued Daniel Atijas, that I had never once invited him to see my paintings, and the thought had stung him like a lash. He had been sitting in the living room of the home of the director of the Literary Arts Programs, where he was sipping Ceylonese tea with the director's wife, when one of them mentioned me in passing. The wife of the director of the Literary Arts Programs remarked that I was known for my "broad sweeps." What are "broad sweeps"? asked Daniel Atijas, and how could it be that I had never offered to show him my works? I don't know why he felt the need to refer to my paintings as works — he didn't look like the type who so readily forgets the words for things — but I was no longer sure of anything. Had I been able to, I would have melted under the rays of the sun, which was somewhere high in the sky, up above, covered at times by clouds, as could be seen by the shadows that occasionally slid over the conifers and the studios. I took a step somehow to the side instead of forward, but I had to move if I wanted to speak, and I told him I had no explanation for it, that some things happen despite our best intentions and that regardless of how much we take part in them, we can only watch ourselves from the sideline as if we were a stranger. Daniel Atijas said this was silly, that nothing, nothing at all, happens despite our will, for which there was solid proof, he said, though he didn't give a single example but instead explained that he was loath to contradict me, which flew in the face of all of his convictions, but we had so little time left and shouldn't be wasting it on squabbles; we should be talking instead about how we'd spend tomorrow with Ivan Matulić's grandson. I could have turned and left, I was so infuriated by the mention of the grandson, but there was already a lot of passion in that little space out in front of my studio. Instead, as if repeating the secret signal, I patted my pocket, pulled out my key chain, and moved toward the door. I had nothing to fear: the drawings were tucked away in the pad in the corner, safe behind a pile of canvases, and only with a thorough search—which there was no call for, nor would such a thing even occur to Daniel Atijas, he's not that type of person, or, I corrected myself, he didn't look like that type of person—could the drawings be found. Daniel Atijas followed me, came up the steps, waited for me to unlock the door, then cautiously, when I opened the door, stepped into the studio as if he were fearful of knocking something over. I offered him coffee; he asked for a glass of water. I didn't know what he expected to see, but he seemed disappointed. The smile with which he entered and with which, I'm convinced, he meant to greet the teeming chaos of creativity, slowly faded. He turned around once more, cast a glance over the only paintings he could see, hung on opposite walls, one exactly across from the other, and he came over to *A Rainy Day on the Prairie*, right up to the canvas until his nose was almost touching the layers of paint. The other one, I later explained, had the title *A Bad Day for a Reaper*, and a reaper, in a light-blue worker's overall, reclining on a lounge chair, was watching a combine in the middle of a grain field. His face was reflected on the blade of the scythe on his lap: the left side of his face, his bushy eyebrows, his cheek bristly with stubble, and a bead of sweat there, transparent and slighty irregularly dented, whose convoluted surface exactly reflected the red combine. I do not believe Daniel Atijas noticed this little game, this multiplication of reflections, for he spent less than a minute standing in front of the painting, actually both paintings, long enough to praise my ability, as he put it, to remove the barriers between different levels of reality but not long enough to convince me that he was genuinely interested. He still wanted to know, he said, what the "broad sweeps" were that the wife of the director of the Literary Arts Programs had spoken of, for though he couldn't, with confidence, say what this had meant to him when he heard it, clearly these paintings, despite all their qualities and unusual angles of observation, were no groundbreaking novelty, which, he said, as far as he was concerned, would be the only sweep that would allow movement sideways or forward. I don't understand, I said, how "sweep," which is more evocative of a movement to the right or left of center, could also suggest forward movement, but her words, I said, remind me of the time when I was painting barns and grain silos for hardly any money. Even now, I said, if he were to come to Saskatchewan, he would be able to see several of my "broad sweeps," almost always painted with a nod to socialist realism: men in rubber boots, women in head scarves, everywhere sheaves of grain and machine parts. I always feel that the cogs and flywheels lying about are highly subversive in Soviet realism because they look more like the unreal flying objects in the surreal paintings of Magritte and Dalí than they do like tools, and I still cannot understand, I said, why the censors never banned them. Because, said Daniel Atijas, fantasy, a reality above reality, never bothered them; they had Gogol, after all, and those other writers — he couldn't remember the names — who, and one can say this freely, had a decisive impact on defining literary fantasy; what they, meaning the censors, he said, didn't like were attempts at depicting another, parallel reality, another face of the reality in which they actually lived, which, in essence, was more fantastic in its illusion than any of Gogol's stories. Anyone who had lived under communism, as, for instance, he had, said Daniel Atijas, laying his hand on his chest, will understand this process of an ongoing simulation of reality, a process in which nothing, in the end, is real, nothing is what it seems, nothing has a right side, only a wrong side. But let's drop the question of communism, he said, whose trajectory is on the wane, though he did hope it would not vanish from the earth, because that would knock the world out of kilter, disrupt its equilibrium, an imbalance that had been in evidence since the crash of communist ideology, and though one could still speak of the world's being slightly askew, it had not turned completely upside down, as it surely would were that to happen. I did not entirely agree with him, but at that moment it didn't occur to me to invoke Marx, Lefebvre, Marcuse, or anyone else of the old guard, though had I done so, I know it would have been a big surprise for him. I had no idea, to be fair, what to say. I said nothing. Somehow I had imagined this differently: his visit to the studio, a viewing of the drawings, the story of the maturation of the face, his face, of course, but also mine, because what was surfacing under my brush or pencil belonged to me, too—it was mine as much as his—and then us conversing in hushed whispers, as if we weren't alone, as if those faces on the drawings were real around us, which perhaps was not far from the truth, especially when one has in mind that each person is actually a multitude of people and hence a multitude of faces, some of which are totally unlike the others. Instead of that, Daniel Atijas began talking about the threads, which he said could explain to him and me, as if I cared, the failure of Ivan Matulić's grandson to catch on to what was going on behind the simulation of the new Croatian reality. He could speak in the same vein, he continued, about the simulation of the new Serbian reality, or any reality in the region of what used to be his country, since there was no difference among them: all those new realities were founded on the tried-and-true mechanism of simulating communist reality, so to reference one implied all the others, but the facts from the story that Ivan Matulić's grandson told us, the place-names, events, and names of people, were keeping him in that context. This does not mean, he said, that any one part of the former whole is better than any other, nor does it mean that any part is worse. He was sure, he said, that all the parts were equal, and at the time right before and immediately after the breakup they were doing nothing more than switching one simulated reality for another. The difference, he said, is in how long each of these newly simulated realities persisted, and with the exception of the northernmost and southernmost parts of his former country, they were still right there. It wouldn't surprise him, said Daniel Atijas, if I couldn't follow what he was saying, which was, in fact, the case, both because of my poor knowledge of the historical and geographic details of his former country and because of my unarticulated but no less real refusal to face the truth of how I had gambled away the chance I had been waiting for all these days. I can see now that while he was talking about the simulating of reality in his former country I was simulating reality in my studio, trying to convince myself that things would be playing out in a way they never would. I did not admit to him that I didn't understand what he was saying, though I did admit to having troubles, but he, I added, should ignore them. He did not. He spent the next forty minutes, if not longer, setting out the way he saw Ivan Matulić's grandson's lack of compass, not stopping for a moment to consider my approval or possible disagreement. What had, in short, played the greatest part in diverting Ivan Matulić's grandson onto the wrong path, according to Daniel Atijas, was his conviction that what was taking place in Croatia was real change. He could not have known that the new government was using the wiles of the old government to simulate a new reality and attempting to conceal the truth of what was really happening. A simulation of triumph, a simulation of democracy, masked the truth of the absence of democracy, complicity in war crimes, the collapse and ruin of the middle classes, the absence of any willingness to ease ethnic conflict, exactly, said Daniel Atijas, as the new government in Serbia did. Having arrived in Croatia, Ivan Matulić's grandson had no idea that he was moving through a territory that wasn't really there, a reality suspended like stage sets in a theater. No one told him, Daniel Atijas was convinced, for the only people who could have told him were people who had lived behind what they called the Iron Curtain, not the political emigrants and insurgents who fled right after World War II and for whom return meant only one thing: revenge. Besides, as a person who had grown up in the context of a North American view of the world, Ivan Matulić's grandson believed that what you see is what you get, said Daniel Atijas, whereas any child born under eastern European communism would immediately say that never, never must one take what one sees for granted. When Ivan Matulić's grandson finally understood this, and when he saw the reality behind the illusion, or at least sensed the true face of the reality of the new-old Croatia, he was immediately ready to abandon everything, which he did, said Daniel Atijas, but not without consequences. The false reality, or rather insight into its perverted structure, inevitably requires a reexamination of the historical perspective, the historical bases on which reality rests, and once one enters, Daniel Atijas remarked, there is no way out.

Having shaken his reality, Ivan Matulić's grandson razed the past and plucked the veil from distorted history, or at least from the version of history that had been shown to him as uncontrovertibly true. And so it was that he found himself in the middle of a country to which his heart still belonged, a country that was hemorrhaging badly, no doubt about it, but which now stretched out before him in all the poverty of its historical legacy, showing itself as a morass of outdated ideologies, Ustasha crimes, and guilty consciences. This comparison was not, perhaps, the best, said Daniel Atijas, but it was all he could think of: what happened to Ivan Matulić's grandson was like being a groom who has found out, just when he should be tenderly kissing the pursed lips of his bride, that she slit the throat of her previous husband. This gives the groom, said Daniel Atijas, two options: he can keep on his trajectory toward the bride's lips, hoping that the gods will favor him, or he can run as fast as his feet carry him, which, by all counts, is what Ivan Matulić's grandson did. But love had already nestled into his heart, and there, like a worm, it continued to unnerve him, driving him, the grandson — not the worm — to question himself, to doubt his every choice, to keep coming back, to blame himself for things he hadn't done. He became, said Daniel Atijas, a culprit with no guilt, a criminal without a crime, an executioner with no sacrificial victim. Something that seemed at first like a well-intentioned adventure, a jaunt that could bring him nearer to those he was distant from, including members of his family, turned, despite all generic rules, into a tale about a fall, a horror story, an endless silence from which no voices could be enticed. He couldn't speak for me, said Daniel Atijas, but for himself he was sure that such a spiritual condition could not last long, especially when, as with Ivan Matulić's grandson, he found himself in a situation for which he was not responsible, in which he had done nothing wrong. I didn't know what to tell him, just as I didn't know whether, with these words, he meant to justify Ivan Matulić's grandson or, possibly, to blame him. Ignorance, and Daniel Atijas accepted this, was no excuse; not knowing does not mean being free of responsibility; intending is sometimes the same as doing. I had nothing new to say, and there was nothing new that could be said. I didn't want to say anything. All I wanted was to keep my mouth shut, and if there was something that didn't compel me, if there was a story, at least as far as I was concerned, it was over, and it was the story of Ivan Matulić's grandson. And besides, despite all my efforts to follow the details as closely as I could, despite the hours and hours we had spent together, sober and drunk, I was still missing meanings that the two of them, sometimes without a word, were perfectly attuned to. Daniel Atijas interpreted my silence as a sign of continued interest, and he went on about the skewed nature of the world into which, as into the world beyond the looking glass, Ivan Matulić's grandson had stepped. The first thing that was skewed, in Daniel Atijas's opinion, was the trajectory of time along which Ivan Matulić's grandson traveled, and that was the inevitable reflection of something else that was skewed, the time frame of fifty years back, when the ideological impact of a state was measured by its insistence on the eradication of everyone who stood apart, either through religion or ethnicity, from the majority of inhabitants. To mask this distortion, for there was no place in current time for such a position and its consequences, there had to be an additional skewing of the time trajectory, explained Daniel Atijas. So the crimes that were happening now were accorded greater value than the crimes that had happened before. The regime of one totalitarian system, communism, was seen as having outstripped the earlier totalitarian system, fascism, in its horrors. There was, supposedly, so much evil in communism, said Daniel Atijas, that everything else paled by comparison, not only in Croatia but elsewhere in his former country. Hence Ivan Matulić's grandson at first really believed he was doing something for the good of the newly minted state, forged in the glow of a terrible ordeal, but later, once he stopped heeding his heart and began listening to reason, he realized that neither partly nor wholly had this state yet emerged from its previous ordeal. Everything had become so tangled that I could barely keep myself from begging him to stop, though I have to admit I was far more vexed by the passion with which he was telling me all this than I was by the complexities. This passion was so boundless, I thought, in comparison with what I had seen, while we were standing out in front of the studio, in that segment of his sentence in which he had declared his resolve to wait no matter what. The thrill I had felt faded now like a sheet of paper in the sun, yellowed and brittle. That was when Daniel Atijas declared that we should spend the next day together on an outing. He had talked, he said, with the Japanese artists, and they had suggested several attractive destinations. In that case, I said, they are the ones who should go with you. I didn't even try to hide the disappointment in my voice. Indeed, answered Daniel Atijas, he had asked them that straightaway, but it turned out they had another firm commitment, which was a shame, he added, because it would surely be best to go with someone who already knew the lay of the land and the paths, but he had purchased the necessary maps and guides, and during the evening he was planning to study them, so as soon as Ivan Matulić's grandson arrived, and that should be right after breakfast, we'd be ready to set out. Perhaps I should have left the pad with the drawings out in the open, I thought, but that change was not possible. To be frank, I didn't want to make the change, though something along those lines had occurred to me several times. I could only chastise myself. Had someone hinted to me only ten minutes ago that I would be eager to see Daniel Atijas leave my studio, I would have laughed, but now I had to turn away to the window to hide the twitching of my cheek and jaw muscles, a sure sign of fraying patience. It takes so much time to build and so little time to tear down, says one of Mark Robinson's poems, and now that line shone somewhere in the back of my consciousness. Who could have guessed, I thought, that I'd find comfort in one of Mark's poems? I suddenly wanted Daniel Atijas to leave my studio quickly and for it to get dark quickly, and then I wanted to go to a theater and watch a movie about a natural disaster. The quantity of human tragedy in movies like that always pushed me to feel embarrassed by the niggling troubles that I imbued with meaning and which plagued my life. It used to be, in that same mood, I would go to a performance of a Shakespeare play, but then I got tired of how every single character in these plays, even the greatest fool, was always so wise. What I needed were the trite phrases of a Hollywood blockbuster, not the high-flying wisdom of the Stratford bard. It turns out that at that same moment Daniel Atijas, too, was thinking of heights, though not of the human spirit but of the surrounding Rocky Mountains. His first idea, he said, had been for us to climb the highest nearby peak, allowing us, at least temporarily, to distance ourselves from the human race. Afterward he realized that this would require skills none of us probably had, and there wasn't enough time left, at least for him, to make headway in the fundamentals of alpine climbing, so he decided to take the well-traveled road, so to speak, and chose a route that was challenging and yet accessible to all of us right near Banff. The effort we would make to conquer its heights, he said, would be his symbolic yet real farewell to the Art Centre while at the same time it would foreshadow his return to his country, the effort he would need to adjust again to life there. He doubted that I would be able to grasp, he said, what this stay, the twelve or thirteen days that he had spent in Banff, had meant. He himself couldn't fully grasp their real meaning; perhaps the meaning would open up for him only when he started to wish for what was no longer within reach and rail at himself for all he had failed to do. It needn't be something big, he said; little things are what make us what we are. For instance, he said, he hoped he would still have time to get over to the store on the Banff main street, somewhere near the beginning, where he had seen a little onyx owl, and to the museum dedicated to First Nations history and culture. He had cradled the owl twice in his hands, but both times he had put off the purchase, and who knew whether he'd still have time to buy it, just as he didn't know, he said, whether he'd have a chance to visit the First Nations museum, even though he'd set out several times from the Centre with what had seemed like an unshakeable determination to go through the museum with great attention to detail. Our lives, he said, are based on perpetual dispersion, our inability to follow forever the threads we have chosen to follow, and our readiness to blame others for this. How many times, he asked, had I blamed myself for a failing, and how many times had I blamed others? I couldn't come up with an answer to such a tricky question, but he didn't stop looking at me until I said the first numbers that popped into my head. There was a time when I blamed myself, I said, and there were a hundred times when I looked to blame others. Daniel Atijas beamed as if we had reached some terribly important truth. The same was true of him, he said, though he was, perhaps, more inclined to self-accusation, which could be, he said, a reflection of his background, but in most cases, as with me, he said, he would blame others and close his eyes to his own shortcomings. So as far as tomorrow was concerned, he said, he didn't want to leave anything to chance, and all afternoon, and even into the night, if necessary, he intended to dedicate himself to preparations for their outing. He started for the door, turned, and once more surveyed the studio. He kept having this feeling, he said, somewhere at the back of his mind, that we had missed something. He didn't know what, but the absence was there, it was real, so he figured, he said, that there had to be something left unsaid or unviewed. I shook my head. I don't believe I convinced him, but soon afterward he left. I could have breathed a sigh of relief, or I could have wept. I did neither. I went to the corner where the pile of canvases lay, moved them over, and pulled out the pad with the drawings in it. So much effort, I thought, for naught. It didn't matter that it wasn't the truth, for never is any effort a waste — I have always subscribed to that idea. Effort may merely change a drawing's shape or structure, its color, its aggregate condition, but the matter itself, the quantity of matter, remains unchanged. Even if I were to burn all the drawings, they would still exist, at least in the number of molecules, elementary particles, or whatever it is that everything is made of. Just as a word that has once been uttered can never be silenced, no matter how silent one is afterward, so it is that a drawing which has once been put on paper can never be entirely erased. That notion still might not stop me from destroying the drawings, but it alerted me to something else: that I would never be able to destroy them in me. In a few days' time, Daniel Atijas would be strolling the streets of his city again, yet at the same time he would be walking along the path that leads to my studio; he'll be there, talking about how he had met interesting, though naive, Canadians here, yet his voice will still be echoing over the waters of the Bow River, and wild birds will be listening to the inscrutable tales of local Yugoslav politicians; someone will knock at his door, and he will, I am certain, open the door quickly, but here that will not happen, and whoever knocks here will stop, hesitating, after the fifth or sixth tap of a crooked finger, and think that perhaps he should lean his ear to the door. Nothing, only silence. Most often it doesn't matter where a person is, I thought; it matters much more where he is not. The art of absence, I felt like saying, is more important than the skill of presence. Showing up at the right moment, I said, is worth less than a no-show at the right moment. My voice sounded fragile and hollow in the empty studio, like the croak of a frog. True, I thought, it is good at times to be an enchanted frog, especially when a person knows for certain that he will find a prince or princess who will not be squeamish. I attempted to find the right order for the drawings—not chronological, naturally, because there is nothing simpler than laying out a chronology, but instead an order that gradually, with barely visible gradation, led to the acquisition of a broader and, I hoped, more profound insight into the meaning of what the face was or could be. I wasn't certain whether I was actually ordering the drawings to see something that had earlier eluded me or to squelch in myself the thought of destruction, but the work slowly absorbed me, pulled me away from everything else, and when I looked up, I saw the shadows of twilight advancing. I couldn't believe it, because that would mean that I had spent five, maybe six, hours engrossed in mastering the structure of the given form, so I opened the door, and out I went but—no doubt about it: darkness was silting in among the conifers, thinly still, though nearer the forest floor along the path it had already started thickening. Wonder of wonders, I was not hungry, though I couldn't remember when I'd last eaten. I went back to the studio, clicked on the light, switched on the electric stove, and put the teapot on. The drawings were on the table, arranged finally in an order that led in a trajectory toward greater openness, so that the first drawing, the one on the top, showed only a single line, and the last, on the bottom, depicted the entire face. Several drawings on the bottom, perhaps the last six, showed the whole face, of course, but I had succeeded, or at least I believed I had succeeded, in pinpointing the subtle differences that led from the first of them to the last, which was, at the same time, the final drawing made, the end of it all and the beginning of everything else, as I had read on the spine of a book many years ago. I put a teabag into a cup and poured hot water over it. The teabag floated for a moment on the surface and then began to sink, leaving behind it a reddish swirl as if it were burning. I shouldn't have been thinking of fire, incompatible as it is with water, I should have been thinking of blood, a trace of blood, undulating and lithe in the water currents, like the liquid around it in part, but still distinct. I thought, however, that I should go to Daniel Atijas's room, lean my ear against the door, and listen to hear if he was really there, as he had promised, or out roaming through the Art Centre and Banff, attempting, finally, before his departure, to become somebody else. And I did leave the studio, leaving the drawings piled out on the tabletop, because there was no longer any need, I told myself, to stow them away, but I did not go to Lloyd Hall, where our rooms were; instead I headed deeper into the woods until I found myself surrounded by total darkness. The time has come, I thought, to admit that I have lost. I could not remember what it was I had lost, but that was not what mattered; the point was the act of losing, the feeling that something had been permanently taken away and would never come back. I cannot say how long I stayed in the darkness, in the underbrush, among the pines. When I finally returned, I didn't stop till I reached my room. I took off all my clothes, lay down, lifted my arms over my head, and sank into sleep before the sheets had time to get warm. I got up several times that night: twice because of bladder pressure, once because of a dream so real that I had to tell myself, mid-dream, to wake up, and once because of a feeling, which proved false, that someone was sitting on my legs. The dream had to do with something that happened years ago, and while I waited, lying on my back, to go back to sleep, I couldn't find any points in common with what had just happened, unlike what I understood about the feeling of weight on my shins, which I was certain was a sign of the presence of Daniel Atijas's astral body in my room. When I opened my eyes, I couldn't see anything, and I wasn't sure whether astral bodies leave a trace. The weight had, meanwhile, let up, though a mild pain kept hovering around my shins, preventing me from sinking into sleep. Outside, it was almost light. The depth and sharpness of the azure of the sky promised a beautiful day, as I could tell from experience, which, under any other circumstances, would have delighted me and hurried me along through the getting-up and morning rituals, but this morning I had been hoping for rain, and I took the promise of the beauty of the day as betrayal. Then the phone rang. I reached over, picked up the receiver, said hello. There was still a chance that something might change, that some little wheel might slip from the pre-set trajectory of the world. For a moment there was nothing audible in the receiver, and then a man's voice apologized, said it was the wrong number, and hung up. I was convinced that the voice belonged to Ivan Matulić's grandson, that he had found a way to persuade the staff members at the Art Centre switchboard to connect him so early to one of the guests but by mistake had given my room number instead of Daniel Atijas's. I put the receiver back in the cradle, pressed my left hand to my chest, and did what I could to calm the pounding of my heart. To no avail, of course, because the heart does what it will, regardless of what we offer it as a measure of love or hope. I longed for the phone to ring again, to have the voice make the same mistake; and this time I'd listen carefully to be sure it was Ivan Matulić's grandson. Nothing happened except my eyelids growing heavy, so I had to get up to escape slipping back into sleep. On my way to the bathroom my heart stopped pounding, which made it possible to urinate in peace, though afterward I had to wipe two drops of urine off my left thigh with a tissue. Our agreement from yesterday had been to meet for breakfast at nine o'clock sharp. Ivan Matulić's grandson needed less than an hour and a half to drive from Calgary to Banff, which meant, as I confirmed with a quick glance at the clock, that he would be setting out soon. I looked at myself in the mirror, tucked my hair behind my ears, then stuck out my tongue and examined it carefully. Someone told me or I read somewhere that the tongue is the most reliable indicator of changes in the functioning of the human organism, but though I had been staring at its reflection for years, I had learned nothing from it yet. I remembered how one of Nabokov's characters had arrived at similar insights after carefully studying his excrement, but I had never been able to persuade myself to do that, and I always lowered the lid on the toilet bowl before I flushed. I laced up my hiking boots, packed a light jacket in my backpack, tossed in a pair of clean socks, and though all that didn't take long, I was late by the time I got to the dining hall. Daniel Atijas was already seated at the table eating cornflakes and leafing, as I later saw, through a book with descriptions of mountain trails in Banff and the surrounding area. Without taking off my backpack I took two rolls, a pat of butter, and a little packet of honey, put them on a tray, took them to the table where Daniel Atijas was sitting, went back for coffee and again for sugar, and then sat down. All that time Daniel Atijas hadn't looked up from his book. He'd lick his finger, turn the page; sometimes he'd flip to the index at the back or to the table of contents at the beginning. I sliced open the roll, spread the left half with butter and the right half with honey, then put them back together and took a bite. Crumbs dropped to the table, some floated to the floor, one bounced as far as the edge of Daniel Atijas's book. A voice behind me mentioned stars, but when I turned, I didn't see anyone. Daniel Atijas lifted his hand slowly up and behind his head, thrust it under his collar, and scratched. The dining room filled, it got noisier, and just as I had begun to hope that Ivan Matulić's grandson wouldn't show, there he was. He was wearing a plaid shirt, jeans, walking shoes, and a cloth hat. He refused the breakfast that Daniel Atijas offered him. He said he had had a coffee with a lot of milk on his way while driving, and that would hold him until noon, and then, he said, he'd have the sandwich he'd brought. In fact he'd brought two sandwiches, he said, but he was sure he'd only be able to eat one, and if that was the case, he said, he'd be glad to give one of us the other. As he was saying this he was looking at me as if everyone knew I was the one with the voracious appetite. If I'm not mistaken, Daniel Atijas only then looked up from reading his guidebook. Ivan Matulić's grandson did not sit. He stood by the table, shifting from foot to foot, and every so often he raised his shoulders to keep his backpack from slipping any further. He did take off his hat and crumple it up in his hands. The waiter raised the coffee pitcher high in the air as if he were selling it at auction, and when the three of us shook our heads, he moved over to a table where artists from Mexico were sitting. Ivan Matulić's grandson asked what trail we had chosen. He kept looking at me, though I was not the person who should be answering. I didn't know anything either, though I did realize a little later that he must have known something, since he had come all ready for mountain climbing, which he could have known only if he had spoken earlier with Daniel Atijas. Never, I thought, is one act of betrayal enough; it is merely an introduction to a whole series of other betrayals, perfectly tucked one inside the next like those little Russian dolls that create a semblance of an endless series.

Nothing told me what I should do, or rather whether I should do anything. Perhaps it would have been easier for me if Ivan Matulić's grandson had taken a seat, but he kept stubbornly standing, so I got a crick in my neck. The waiter went in the opposite direction, muttering something under his breath. He had thought for a long time, said Daniel Atijas, about where it would be best for us to go and had been torn between Johnston Canyon and one of the trails near Canmore, and he finally realized, he said, that in a day or two he'd be leaving here and he might never, hard as it was for him to say this, return to Banff, so this outing of ours into the mountains was a perfect chance for him to see once more, probably for the last time, some of the scenes that had made the greatest impression on him. Neither Ivan Matulić's grandson nor I said anything. And besides, Daniel Atijas went on, he realized that so far he hadn't, as is so often the case, seen what was nearest: Tunnel Mountain, on whose slopes the Centre stood, and so he'd decided, he said, that we would hike to its summit, where, the guidebook said, there was a beautiful view of the valley of the Bow River and the popular geological formations, the hoodoos, which, from the moment he first had seen them, had stayed with him. I was the first to nod, and then Ivan Matulić's grandson said he agreed and that, faced with the same dilemma, he, too, would have chosen that trail. He had also read, said Daniel Atijas, that there was no tunnel through the mountain despite its name. When they were laying the plans in the late nineteenth century for a route to connect the eastern, Atlantic coast with the western, Pacific coast, said the guidebook, the first version of the plans included boring a tunnel through the mountain, but a better route was found, longer but much less expensive and less arduous to build. The tunnel, it said, was never broached, yet the mountain kept its name, so in a symbolic sense there was some sort of passage there, though no one could traverse it. I interjected that this was the best possible outcome because Tunnel Mountain was sacred to the local Indians, who called it Mountain of the Sleeping Buffalo, and we could only imagine, I said, how much desecration would have resulted from boring such a tunnel. It would be tantamount, I said, to boring a hole through Buddha's belly. The world is a crazy place, said Daniel Atijas, but luckily for all of us, it is not that crazy. I disagreed. I didn't believe this to be a case of the triumph of reason; it was mere coincidence, and if no one had come up with an alternate route or had discovered such a route too late, we would now have a hollow mountain, and the whole region would look completely different. But how would I react, asked Daniel Atijas, to the claim that coincidence is the only true trajectory of fate, that fate is not determined by repetition and inevitability but by sudden departures from the predictable, by the addition of things that are new? Ivan Matulić's grandson was still standing there; he had even begun scraping his shoes on the floor, making no bones about his impatience. I said I wouldn't be able to answer that question, especially not right now, so early in the morning, and just when I smiled at Ivan Matulić's grandson, we were getting ready to go. Daniel Atijas replied that he could not believe I was dismissing so lightly something that, he was profoundly convinced, lay at the heart of artistic creation, of inspiration itself. Artistic creation, he said, is routine, like any job, and that was something, he believed, everyone would agree with. The writer writes, he said, just the way an official enters data into a form or certifies a form with the proper stamp; the musician transcribes parts of his symphony just the way a typesetter sets parts of a text; and the painter fills in the blank spaces on the canvas just the way a gardener pursues harmony in his flower beds. Creativity, he said, is everyday labor, nothing more—a job that may last for years, decades, and which produces, at intervals, books, paintings, sculptures, and concerts, among which there are those that are exceptionally successful, but they are all products of routine, subject to simple analysis. Only certain moments, he said, and only some of the artists, thanks to chance, leap out of the well-oiled system that manufactures, one might say, artworks like refrigerators or automobiles on an assembly line, and that is when works are created that elude all classification, he said, and become the basis for a new system. I couldn't understand why he wanted to talk about this just then, why he wasn't paying attention to the tormented expression of Ivan Matulić's grandson, who clearly could find no point of contact between what Daniel Atijas was talking about and our climbing Tunnel Mountain. Our civilization, said Daniel Atijas, and each one of us as an individual, as artist or ordinary person, whatever, develops that way, he said, in leaps, from one coincidence to another, but no one can say when or whether the coincidence will happen. There are writers, he said, who write appealing, popular books their whole lives, though not a single one of the books steps outside the limits of what is already known, and they, these writers, have earned a prominent place in literature, but their impact is an impact with no genuine value: they have come into the world and left it, and nothing actually happened as a consequence. Isn't that how it is with all of us? I asked. Do we not all leave this world as if we had never been here, regardless of whether we lived on the plains or among mountains? Ivan Matulić's grandson sighed loudly, the way every weary person does, and at that moment I clearly saw that my sympathies, if Daniel Atijas were to keep droning on about creative drives, might well shift over to the grandson's side, which, I admit, surprised me so much that I felt a sort of shock, as when a source of very weak current zaps your fingers. I proposed that we leave the conversation about the meaning of creativity and the system of the world for the hike up Tunnel Mountain, or maybe for the descent, since one breathes with more difficulty while climbing, and an overabundance of words might disturb the already-jagged rhythm of breathing, while on the way down words flow like a torrent. I wasn't sure whether Daniel Atijas would accept this; he didn't strike me as the type who gives up easily—he looked like a person who might, on the surface, give up, but not really, on the inside—but it was too late for me to change anything. Daniel Atijas took out a map of Banff and its surroundings, pushed aside the cups and saucers, and spread it out on the table. We all leaned over the map. For a while we said nothing and looked it over while our heads almost touched. One of the three of us was breathing more hastily and jerkily than the others, but I wasn't sure who. Daniel Atijas placed his finger on the Art Centre and drew it along Saint Julian Road all the way to a place, roughly between Wolf and Wolverine Streets, where, he said, the trail that led to the summit of Tunnel Mountain began. Before that, however, he said, we had to make sandwiches. Ivan Matulić's grandson already had sandwiches and a plastic bottle of water in his backpack, so it was up to me to go and get four rolls, a handful of thinly sliced Trappist cheese, and several pats of butter. While I was spreading food on the gaping halves, I remembered how we had gone the first time on Sunday a week ago to walk along the river and have a look at the hoodoos, and how Daniel Atijas had rolled their name around in his mouth as if chewing gooey caramel. I hadn't told him then that some Native Americans believed they were actually tepees, Indian tents in which dwelt evil gods, but it suddenly occurred to me that he had been talking at that point about coincidence in nature in an entirely different way, not praising it, as he had done just now, which had also surprised me, because I had been convinced, who knows why, that Daniel Atijas possessed a remarkably firm and precise system of intellectual references, a system in which there were no errors, or at least the likelihood of any coming up was minimal. I was so caught up in these thoughts that Ivan Matulić's grandson had to tap me on the shoulder to get my attention. He was still standing by the table, and now and then, with one hand or both, he'd lean on it. He asked what I wanted to drink during our walk: water or, like Daniel Atijas, a soda? We may, I said then, possibly be overdoing it with all these preparations, since I know the trail, and all we need for our climb to the top of Tunnel Mountain is some thirty minutes, forty at the outside, certainly less than an hour. True, said Daniel Atijas, this is not a great distance; he knew that the whole trail was about a mile and a half long and that the difference in elevation was about nine hundred feet, but his idea hadn't been so much about the walking or hiking, and even less about the distance and the effort, as about the possibility of spending the whole day in nature having peaceful conversations the likes of which he would not be able to enjoy once he went back, so soon, to his country. I couldn't say anything to him about that; he was leaving, after all, and I was staying; so I told Ivan Matulić's grandson to take orange juice for me. Ivan Matulić's grandson was a little surprised and asked me whether I was certain about the orange juice, because it always gave him indigestion, and he could drink only two or three sips, sometimes not even that much. Each of us is different, I told him, and what makes one person weak might make someone else very strong. Ivan Matulić's grandson shrugged, turned, and walked away. Daniel Atijas called after him to remind him to wait for us out in front of the store. He himself went on wrapping sandwiches in napkins and packing them in my backpack. He did it carefully and skillfully, as if he had been doing nothing but that his entire life. I don't remember that I had ever seen him, before that, more absorbed, given over to something extremely unimportant; and as if he had read my thoughts, he said that the beauty of life is hidden in the fullness of every moment, and that every moment should be lived as if there were nothing else. He wrapped the last sandwich, placed it with the others, downed another swig of coffee, and said it was time for us to go. I put on my backpack and turned, then turned again to take a careful look at the surface of the table, checking to see whether we'd forgotten anything. The waiter raised his hand and waved, but when I went to wave back, he had bent over and was brushing crumbs off his pants. I hurried after Daniel Atijas, left the building, and turned the corner, and then I saw them: they were standing facing each other, eye to eye; Ivan Matulić's grandson was speaking steadily, with no vehemence, and Daniel Atijas's left hand rested on his right shoulder. Perhaps I should have turned around then and left, but I went on walking toward them and even pretended not to notice. Sometimes, I told Daniel Atijas not long after we'd met, walking is only a way not to stand still, and as I walked over to them I felt as if I were standing, as if I'd never get there. Ivan Matulić's grandson was the first to notice me, and then Daniel Atijas turned. He had just been talking, he said, about how we mustn't allow any experience to get the better of us, and how in everything we must seek something to hold on to, a handhold or a foothold, no matter how slippery the path might be or how weak the hand or foot. The whole time he wasn't taking his hand off the grandson's shoulder, and he was even squeezing it gently, as I could see, with his fingertips. I looked at my watch but didn't see it. We're running late, I nevertheless said, in an artificial and alarming tone, as if it were nearly nightfall. Daniel Atijas and Ivan Matulić's grandson finally moved apart, and Ivan Matulić's grandson thrust his hand into the backpack at his feet, took out the bottle of orange juice, and handed it to me. I took it carefully, as if it were a hot iron, put it in my backpack, tightened the cord and tied it in a double, lopsided bow, and finally said I was ready for us to go. All of us are ready, said Daniel Atijas, and suddenly a thrill shot through me as if I were part of an expedition to the North or South Pole. I could see it all so clearly: Ivan Matulić's grandson and Daniel Atijas and the people who, having finished with their breakfast, were leaving the dining hall and crossing the street and the whole Centre and myself, all of whom I saw from behind, as if I were watching everything from a foot or so behind my back. There was a harsh light emanating from everything, but the light didn't disperse or spread; it remained as an inch-or-two-wide edging around the contours of the bodies and buildings, reminding me of stories of auras and photographs of plants surrounded by a golden glow. Daniel Atijas and Ivan Matulić's grandson had already walked away, and all I could do was take several unsure steps, but then I had to stop. I needed to go up the dozen steps that led to Saint Julian Road, but I didn't dare move my foot forward and guess where each step ended and the contour of its glaring edge began. I was convinced that if I took just one more step, I would fall, perhaps even tumble into the crack between the real edge and the glaring edge, and no one would be able to fish me out, as if I'd fallen into a crack in a glacier. I took this as the last warning to abandon the hike up Tunnel Mountain and opened my mouth to shout, to call Daniel Atijas and Ivan Matulić's grandson to come back, but when I looked up, I could see that they had already made it to the curve in the road, and, engrossed in their conversation, they couldn't have cared less where I was. I cannot pinpoint exactly what it was I was feeling then. Words like "rage" or "letdown" or "desolation" express nothing to me. Besides, I had no feeling then for words: I was staggering under the weight of pure emotion. Whatever the case, just then the harshly glaring auras faded, and I could mount the stairs and hurry after Ivan Matulić's grandson and Daniel Atijas, that is, hurry to the place where they'd disappeared from sight. And while I was trotting along and my backpack was bouncing on my back, I swallowed saliva full of bitterness, as if I had been chewing a bad-tasting plant from the plains. When I caught up to them, I was so out of breath that all I could do was listen to what they were saying. Only Daniel Atijas was speaking. He was talking in a didactic voice without pause, as if reciting something he knew by heart, and Ivan Matulić's grandson was nodding in assent, though it was immediately clear to me that he gave no credence to what Daniel Atijas was saying. By all indications they were resuming the conversation that had started out in front of the store, or who knows when, for as time passed I was increasingly convinced that Daniel Atijas was leading a different life from the one I had allotted him or attempted to define. At one moment, a few days ago, I had been so certain that he was spending nearly all his free time with me, that he was every bit as devoted to me as I was to him, but now I knew that my attempts to take over his life completely had not worked and, furthermore, that he may not even have noticed what I was up to, and that, in other words, he had never for a moment seen in me someone who was different in any way from the other people he met at the Centre. This was a horrible thought, but sometimes there is no other option, and horror is all, or only, what we get. I should, it seems, have said something about that then, because it might have been more understandable to Ivan Matulić's grandson than what Daniel Atijas was telling him. He was talking about the past, speaking of the need for forgiveness, insisting on the value of truth, but there was nothing practical in it; he was not showing a way to heal, the necessity of acknowledging defeat as the only way to move toward victory. Ivan Matulić's grandson nodded earnestly, which, out of the corner of the eye, in passing, might appear to be a sign of genuine confirmation and rapport, a sign of readiness to embrace the words as they reached him. However, had Daniel Atijas taken a closer look, had he stopped, looked face-on at him, in the eyes, he would have seen that nothing of what he had been saying stuck, that his words were crumbling as soon as they left his lips, and that now, like a fine dust, and of this I was convinced, they were scattered on the ground behind us, coating Saint Julian Road the way leaves cover it in autumn. There is nothing so pathetic, I thought, as a speech by someone who has no faith in words. Perhaps I should have said this aloud; maybe everything would have played out differently had I done that, but I didn't, in fact, want to get embroiled in something which, I was convinced, was in no way mine, and which, to be perfectly frank, I didn't really understand. I remember that during one of our first walks, Daniel Atijas had told me how I should picture a civil war raging in Canada and how my country was disintegrating into noise and fury, but those images, no matter how horrible they were when I pictured them, were not authentic, they did not teach me anything, because in imagined, unlike genuine, experience, the knowledge that what is happening is not real is ever present: there is always an exit. In real experience, I'd said, nothing helps, not dreams or illusions, not shutting one's eyes, and that is where we left it. Daniel Atijas had dismissed this out of hand, I'd shrugged helplessly, a cloud scudded across the sky, an elk rubbed against a tree, tourists clicked their cameras. Remembering that is when it occurred to me that we had never had our picture taken, so I went over to Ivan Matulić's grandson and Daniel Atijas and told them it would be a good idea for me to run back and get my camera, as this would be our last chance to get a picture of us together. Had I known how true this was, I probably would have chosen other words, but at the time, driven by the additional thought of the necessity of destroying all my drawings, I was thinking of the document, of the actual presence of a photograph, of something that could remain as a trace of Daniel Atijas beyond the administrative records of the visit, his lecture, and expenses, and I was therefore poised to race back to my room and even, if need be, to the studio, for I wasn't sure where I had left my camera. But the two of them were adamant. No pictures, they said, no way. And besides, added Daniel Atijas, once a person departs, it is a bad idea to return. That confused me because he did not strike me as the type of person who would buy into such superstitions, though, I thought, if people do come to Banff to become somebody else, maybe this simply confirms the subversive power of the Rocky Mountains. What I mean to say is that from the very start I believed Daniel Atijas to be an extremely rational person, which is why, after all, and this I knew, he could not understand the collapse of his country, which was irrational and defied all logic. It is easiest, he had said at the lecture, to refer to the inevitability of history, but history, like fate, is not inevitable; exactly like fate, it is the result of free choice. When I asked him several days later to explain what he'd meant, he refused, justifying himself with the claim that no matter what we may think of history, once it runs its course, it can never change, which means, he added, that any conversation about it is spurious, as is conversation about fate. I told him I didn't believe in fate, at which he laughed and answered that belief doesn't matter, because lack of belief in fate can't touch fate itself. Fate, he added, is what happens, and since our existence is strung together of things that happen, that means that we exist only in fate, never outside it. This, it seems to me, was when we were standing by the cemetery wall, not the first time but later, when, if I'm not mistaken, we were on our way up the path leading to the Centre. Now all the days seem like a cluster of fleeting moments, but at the time they had length and fullness, and I believed they would never end. The story about fate seems fateful to me now, my disbelief notwithstanding, but isn't that the way it always is? Future events, things that have not yet happened, always imbue the events that have passed with meaning; they become confirmations of something we could never have predicted but which afterward, after the events that are their consequence, seems crystal clear. And that is probably what Daniel Atijas had been meaning to say at one point: the collapse of his country now can and must be seen as the culmination of a series of givens, and history from here on will always be interpreted that way, but each of these givens was preceded by a moment in which someone made a choice which led inexorably to that outcome. In short, whether deliberately or otherwise, fate did not allow us to have our picture taken. We proceeded along Saint Julian Road, one behind the other, in a row, as if we were already on the mountain trail. Ivan Matulić's grandson led the way, Daniel Atijas was behind him, and I was last. Occasionally a car would pass us, and we met cyclists in black shorts wearing red helmets. I spotted a squirrel but didn't mention it. I wanted to reach the beginning of the trail as soon as possible, in hopes, I guess, that the feeling of there being a goal, even if it was the summit of the mountain, would be welcome for all of us, especially me. Daniel Atijas had meanwhile taken his guidebook out of his pocket again, and in a solemn voice he announced that now we were at an elevation of over thirty-nine hundred feet, and that when we reached the highest point of our climb we would be at nearly fifty-one hundred feet. Nothing special, I told him, compared to the other peaks in the Rocky Mountains, but quite enough for us. Ivan Matulić's grandson replied that as far as he was concerned, he would gladly stop at the spot where we were standing just then, sit down, and stay there, perfectly still. Daniel Atijas couldn't believe, he said, that we were so willing to give up on a climb that would, as happened every time we neared the sky, bring with it a spiritual upsurge, an ascent into the divine sphere, and cohesion to the soul. Especially as far as I was concerned, he said, turning to look at me, that should be clear, since I came from the plains. We were just reaching a parking lot, where Ivan Matulić's grandson was the first to catch sight of the sign marking the beginning of the trail, and actually I found this welcome, because as it was, I couldn't have come up with a reply to Daniel Atijas's comment. The plains are stifling, on this he and I had agreed long ago, but I was not prepared to embrace the claim without reservation that every ascent of a body implies an ascent of the spirit, that he who lives on a mountain is moving at the same time on spiritual elevations which are inaccessible to people on the plains. Perhaps none of that matters, I thought, especially after my failed attempts yesterday to interpose the face I had been carrying inside me on the face that was standing before me. Daniel Atijas proposed that we wait for a group of walkers who were at the corner of the parking lot to get ahead because he would like, he said, for us to have our peace and quiet while we climbed. Once we set out, he said, we would need to follow our own pace and shouldn't have to adapt to the hurrying or slowing of the group hiking ahead of us. Ivan Matulić's grandson opened his backpack, took out his water bottle, and had a few sips. Then he wiped his mouth with his upper arm and put the bottle back in the pack. The voices of the hikers could no longer be heard, but Daniel Atijas still gave no sign for us to begin. Clouds were moving across the sky, so we were sometimes covered by a pale shadow, though we could feel the warmth of the sun's rays more often. Daniel Atijas looked at his watch and nodded. Ivan Matulić's grandson again led the way, but now I went after him, leaving Daniel Atijas to wrestle with his map as it puffed up with wind while he folded it, and to run after us as if he wanted to conquer the first slope at a jog. Later, once we'd crossed the road with the same name as the mountain, the going got easier, the slope was less steep, the trail meandered gradually, the pines and fir trees gave off a pleasant scent, but before that, while we were still on the first part of the climb, I really thought I'd give up, that I'd plop right down on the ground, just as Ivan Matulić's grandson had wanted to, and slide back downhill to the parking lot. I hoped, of course, that this would convince Daniel Atijas to return, but he quickly passed me, panting, it's true, but not as much as I, and went on hiking right next to Ivan Matulić's grandson. They immediately struck up, or rather resumed, their conversation, picking up, I assume, the threads spun while we were walking along Saint Julian Road, but my lagging, along with my louder and louder panting, meant that all I heard were fragments of sentences, shards of words. Then a darker shadow that looked like a snake forced me to stop altogether, and though I immediately scolded myself for such nonsense, since in Banff at such an elevation there were unlikely to be any reptiles, this little slip in caution contributed to my climbing alone for the next several minutes until I made it up to the road. Daniel Atijas and Ivan Matulić's grandson were waiting for me on the other side, surrounded by a group of Japanese tourists to whom they were trying to explain something. Each of them was holding a map or guidebook, or at least the publication one receives upon entering the Banff National Park, and they were staring at them, trying to decipher the meaning of the instructions they had been given. Then all at the same moment they closed their books and folded their maps, bowed and said thank you, hurriedly crossed the road, and headed down the part of the trail I had just come up. I longed to sit down and catch my breath, but Daniel Atijas and Ivan Matulić's grandson were adamant. Let's keep going, keep going, said Daniel Atijas, as if the fate of the entire world depended on our efforts. Again I considered giving up; it still wasn't too late for such a decision, and I wouldn't have had to go back all the way to the start of the trail, because the road we were on, which had the same name as the mountain, also ran down to the Centre, but then I realized that Daniel Atijas might take that as an affront, as I definitely would have done had I been in his place. He didn't strike me as the type of person who would readily assign cosmic value to things of no importance, but there was no need for me to test that at this moment, when all he had was a day, maybe two, before his departure. Now I can, of course, berate myself for not giving up, but then I simply wished that, despite my disappointments, I could keep our relationship on the best possible terms, and I obediently set out after them, having taken a few sips before that of orange juice. The slope became gentler, the trail meandered among the firs and pines—admittedly a respite of sorts. And besides, we stopped in many places surrounded by shadows and had a look at the views that were spreading before us as on a stage. This revived me, and so I could briskly follow Ivan Matulić's grandson, who was leading the way, and Daniel Atijas, who followed him, peering from time to time into his guidebook. The trail ran along a ridge and then with an altogether gentle slope reached the summit, where once, Daniel Atijas read, there used to stand a lookout post for forest fires. Poring over the map for a while, we figured out which mountains we could see from there, which ranges ran along the horizon, and where the highest peak was, but after the initial thrill, and even a little jostling, our interest waned, and soon we dispersed, each of us looking for something different: Daniel Atijas went back along the ridge, believing he could find a vantage point from which to see the hoodoos, Ivan Matulić's grandson mingled with a group of tourists listening attentively while a woman described the origins of the different geological formations in the Banff area, and I stayed behind to survey the golf course that stretched along the river, unsure about whether I felt it was a perfect adaptation of nature, as it seemed from this height, or a blotch on the natural face of the world. I found an almost-round stone slab and sat on it. Closing my eyes, I began, despite the surrounding voices and noise, to hearken to the altitude. There is something, I thought, that cannot be changed, and that, as I had said to Daniel Atijas, is the feeling of belonging to solitude. The artist who is not alone, I said to him then, is only barely an artist, since the interpretation means more to him than the work itself, which, after all, I made a point of saying, may be of no consequence whatsoever. Daniel Atijas had then drawn my attention to the fact that totalitarian rulers are always alone because the multitude around them is actually invisible, but I never managed to discover any connection between totalitarian rulers and artists. All I meant to say, I then said, is that most of the time an artwork is not created for this or that meaning, as critics, and with them the public, often like to think, but without involving any search for meaning. It is created for itself alone or, possibly, for no reason at all. Why should everything, I asked him, have to have meaning, including meaninglessness itself? Actually I cannot remember exactly when it was that we spoke about that. All those days are merged into an indivisible whole, and sometimes, no matter how hard I try, I cannot draw even the slenderest dividing line between them. I am almost certain, for instance, that Daniel Atijas arrived in Banff on a Tuesday, but I cannot determine whether we were at the party at the home of the director of the Literary Arts Programs on the Saturday or the Sunday, which doesn't maybe matter so much, especially if one is comparing it to other things, though I have noticed many times that the question of what matters—the meaning of an event or person or any apparently insignificant moment— usually arises in and of itself, outside us, and persuades us to give ourselves over to it, and it won't release us until we are satisfied with what we have done. This may have occurred to me while I was sitting on that round slab of stone near the highest point of Tunnel Mountain, soaking in the warmth of the sun's rays until the surrounding clamor died away in my ears, so I thought I was finally hearing silence, silence and nothing but silence: I had fallen asleep. When I first opened my eyes, I didn't realize I had been sleeping. My nap seemed to me but a blink of an eye; I was convinced that my absence from reality couldn't have lasted long. Then I looked around and saw Daniel Atijas and Ivan Matulić's grandson sitting under a pine tree eating their sandwiches, and I was confused for a minute, because the last time I had seen them they had each been somewhere different. I don't know whether they were talking, because even if they were talking, I was too far to hear anything, just as I was too far to make out the expressions on their faces, but I am certain that Ivan Matulić's grandson was holding his head a little bent to the side, the way a person does who is listening attentively. I got up, stretched, yawned, and rubbed my eyes. While I was rummaging through my backpack, all of a jumble, looking for the orange juice, Daniel Atijas noticed my activity and waved. Ivan Matulić's grandson joined him, and for a time there we were, waving to each other atop Tunnel Mountain. It's a good thing, I thought when I turned to look around, that there weren't very many people there just then, because had there been, I wouldn't have known what to do in my embarrassment. Daniel Atijas struck me as the type of person who couldn't have cared less whether he was alone or surrounded by an uncountable multitude: he would always behave in just the same way. But I was always fearful of the possibility that I might become a focus of attention, that of others as well as my own. I tossed the backpack on my back and set off for their pine tree. They were closer to me than they had seemed, a surprise for both me and them, for it was obvious that they had to stop talking quickly when they saw my short, early-afternoon shadow. Ivan Matulić's grandson coughed, cleared his throat, and said they had just been commenting on how every mountain peak is always a summit and how there is not a great difference between being on top of Mount Everest and being on top of Tunnel Mountain. On Everest, he said, you stand above everything, of course, while here, he said, gesturing in a circle, you are beneath everything, because all the surrounding mountains reach higher altitudes, but what matters is the feeling, not the altitude, which is admittedly, he said, a big difference. My gaze followed his finger, pointing to the surrounding mountains, Sulphur and Rundle and the others, but I didn't believe him. Once a person starts doubting, it is easier to doubt than to believe. Daniel Atijas would understand that, though he might not agree, though this no longer interested me. Just in case, I asked them what they had been talking about. They exchanged glances like boys caught out in a lie and said they had been sitting there in silence. They had been waiting, said Daniel Atijas, for me to wake up, because they thought it would be nice for us to have lunch together, but when they saw me still sleeping, they moved away, sat in the shade, took out their sandwiches and juices, he having taken his from my backpack, and started to eat. I had to shove my hands into my pockets so that I wouldn't start waving my arms and shouting, I was so upset by the lie. It's a good thing, I thought, that we aren't on one of those peaks, because now I would definitely die of a lack of oxygen. Ivan Matulić's grandson also shoved his hands into his pockets, though his gesture couldn't have had anything to do with my anger. Coincidences like this happen, whether or not a person believes in chance. Daniel Atijas and I had already talked about that once, I couldn't remember when, but at the moment the conversation seemed so long ago that it ceased existing altogether. While I watched Daniel Atijas and Ivan Matulić's grandson exchanging surreptitious glances, I thought how incredible it was, the ease with which events that were so promising at first, especially those which simultaneously offer undreamed-of ramifications, turn into something that is the opposite, which is most often accompanied by a feeling of betrayal, loss, and— why not?—submission to tragedy. The only consolation in all this is that without it there would be no art, certainly no literature, which, one can freely say, is nourished precisely by such betrayed expectations. In this, I thought, lies the advantage of literature over painting, for what literature can merely suggest by playing with presentiments, painting must articulate fully, except when the painting is based on a myth or historical fact and the observer can take into consideration whatever is left unsaid or undepicted. I assumed that these thoughts were coming to me because I happened to be on a mountaintop, albeit a low-altitude peak, and I felt a pang of sorrow that I couldn't share them with Daniel Atijas, for whom they were intended. Perhaps I could, I thought, take him a little farther from this spot; perhaps I could come up with an excuse which would justify our stepping away from Ivan Matulić's grandson, and then, keeping an eye out the whole time for the grandson and his possible approach, I could repeat it all and, finally, ask the question for which, after all these years, I had yet to come up with an answer: is the edge of the canvas—the perimeter of the picture, its frame—the place where the picture ends or where it begins? Now I wonder why I hadn't thought to ask him that before. It is true that the days we spent together in Banff were crammed with activities, and that sometimes things happened with terrible speed, but there were periods of quiet ease, of a candor that enticed one to engage in just that sort of conversation. Perhaps now I am thinking this way because a person's departure, his absence, prompts examination of his presence, brings up insights about what was missed and regrets that some words were not said instead of others and that some things happened at all. We live, it occurs to me, only so we can constantly rebuke ourselves for what we cannot change. The more a thing cannot be changed, one could say, the more we regret not changing it at a time when change was possible, even though nothing at the time showed us we should. In a certain sense, we expect of life that it changes in and of itself, more or less like the seasons, and therefore most people reach the end of their journey without realizing that they themselves were the real masters of their fate. That thought has always filled me with disgust, the readiness of people to follow the mob, to follow anyone but themselves, and there may be no better place to see this than here in western Canada, where everyone is full of talk about individuality while longing, at the same time, for a political program that will, under the guise of slogans about respect for individual differences, bring them all to uniformity. Perhaps I should have said that out loud, for, who knows, Ivan Matulić's grandson might have recognized himself. Just then he began collecting the crumpled napkins, plastic bags, and water bottles and attempting to organize them in his backpack. So while Ivan Matulić's grandson was tightening the straps, while Daniel Atijas was picking up pebbles and throwing them at a nearby tree, while I was imagining unimaginable things, a black cloud suddenly appeared in the sky. It is really not clear to me where it came from: I looked up and there it was in the sky, directly overhead. It may be that on the plains I was used to storms rising slowly along the line of the horizon, to the upward thrust of a mass of dark clouds until the entire sky was covered, so the speed with which the changes unfolded here caught me by surprise. I looked down at the ground, still hunting for trash, and when I looked up again, the clouds in the sky were roiling as in a cauldron. I assumed they must have come along the same route as the first cloud, but there was no time for guesswork. Several hikers walked by us, moving quickly toward the trail that led downhill. We needed to go with them, I said, but for whatever reason Daniel Atijas and Ivan Matulić's grandson held back. Just as the rain was beginning, it occurred to me that maybe they wanted me to be the first to set off, to leave them behind, which, of course, was the last thing on my mind, so then I began to find reasons to slow down—tying my shoelaces, pretending I had caught sight of an intriguing pebble. The rain pelted harder and the wind picked up, so we were quickly soaked to the skin. I don't know about the others, but my teeth were chattering and my every muscle was shivering so that I could barely walk. We were still on the ridge, only halfway to the meandering trail through the conifer wood where the trees would offer at least some protection, and I suddenly thought we would never get there. The gusts of wind picked up. They lifted the raindrops and flung them in our faces, reducing visibility and darkening the already-shriveling light. Head bent, moving only a step at a time, I saw rivulets of rain slithering through the grass, the low undergrowth, and the rocks. Daniel Atijas was walking a little faster than Ivan Matulić's grandson and me, and he was about thirty feet ahead of us, perhaps, I thought, because he had no backpack. A silly thought, of course, because there was nothing heavy in either of our packs, and buffeted by the gusts, they were swinging freely on our backs. The capacity for one's preoccupation with petty spite is astonishing, even at moments of enormous strain or excitement—preoccupation with the little loathings that have no role other than to poison the soul and erode morale, especially when they remain unspoken. I leaned over even more, as if I could shrink in size or turn into a snail and creep into my shell, and bent over like that, my eyes almost closed, I turned to Ivan Matulić's grandson. I meant to tell him to speed up, that we should catch up with Daniel Atijas and that all of us together, as we had come up, should head down along the trail leading to Saint Julian Road, and it took me several seconds to notice, with my eyes blinded by the wind and rain, that Ivan Matulić's grandson was no longer next to me, to my right, where he had been. I stopped, turned to look the other way, and saw him there. He wasn't nearby but had somehow veered off diagonally with his arms up over his face. To this day I can't be sure whether he left the trail because of his crisscrossed arms—they must have reduced his already-limited field of vision—or, as I am sometimes inclined to believe, he left the trail and then, when he had gotten far enough off, raised his arms to hide the truth from us and, perhaps, himself. None of that matters now, because no matter what was on his mind, it changes nothing. In life, unlike in art, there's no way to go back to the beginning; there is no page to tear out or canvas to paint over. That didn't occur to me just then; nothing occurred to me. When I realized that Ivan Matulić's grandson, whether intentionally or not, was making straight for the edge of a cliff, I drew a blank. I gaped like a fish on dry land, though I was drenched, and I looked over at Daniel Atijas, who seemed to be moving quickly away, then at Ivan Matulić's grandson, also moving away, though more slowly, but in his case, as I now know, velocity was moot. What happened next happened in an instant: a shriek tore from my throat at last; I hurtled, crouching like a sprinter, after Ivan Matulić's grandson; Daniel Atijas stopped, turned, brought his right hand to his eyes as if sun, not rain, were preventing him from seeing, and then he, too, sprinted our way; Ivan Matulić's grandson also turned, perhaps in response to the shriek or maybe because he wasn't certain of his intentions; my foot splashed through a puddle, and the spray, as if in slow motion, rose up fountainlike around me and mingled with the rain; Ivan Matulić's grandson lost his balance or maybe tripped on a rock protruding from the low-growing shrubs, which, a little later, I hopped over, but by then Ivan Matulić's grandson had crashed to the ground and begun rolling and tumbling toward the precipice; I threw myself after him and managed to grab his left hand; I held on to it with my left, but when it slipped through my fingers, I lurched around and grabbed him with my right, meanwhile groping with my left for a support or something to grab; with my chin to the ground I saw Ivan Matulić's grandson's eyes, aghast, and when I turned and lowered my left cheek to the wet earth, I caught sight of Daniel Atijas, pumping his legs high as he ran toward us, his mouth open, no sound reaching us; again I looked at Ivan Matulić's grandson; his body was mostly over the cliff edge by then, out of my sight; I should say something, I thought; and then I let him go. Everything after that happened very fast. Time caught up later. First Daniel Atijas reached me, panting; he touched his face and repeated that this was impossible, though he never once said what. Later it turned out that we had not been alone on the peak, because several hikers approached us, most of them drawn, as one later said, by Daniel Atijas's cries. One of the hikers had a cell phone and called the police. While we were waiting for them, the rain let up, the clouds dispersed, the sun came out. A woman peered over the cliff edge, but there was nothing, she said, to see, or rather, she said, she could see all sorts of things but no body. I was tired, my knees shivered but I didn't want to sit down. It seemed inappropriate somehow, and besides the ground was wet. When the police got there, they brought in a special rescue team, a group of mountaineers, who, after I showed them the precise spot where it had all happened, found the body of Ivan Matulić's grandson. While we waited for them to prepare everything necessary for lowering the stretcher, I spoke with two police officers.

Really, I talked with only one; the other did nothing the whole time but nod as if approving my every word. They also talked with Daniel Atijas, and he, I heard, confirmed what I'd said, remarking that even from a distance, even at a run, it was possible to see, he said, that I had poured every atom of strength into holding on to Ivan Matulić's grandson before he plunged to his death. He hadn't known then, he said, that this would end in death, of course, but the moment he realized it, when, he said, he saw our hands pulling apart, he could only regret that he hadn't been three or four steps closer once he started running. Had he been closer, he said, this whole story would have had a different ending. The police officer thanked us and, seeing that the mountaineers had brought in the stretcher, asked if we could identify the victim. I refused, pleading distress, but Daniel Atijas followed the police officer, went to the stretcher, leaned over, and lifted the corner of the white sheet. He looked away. Yes, said Daniel Atijas, that's him. Soon after that, if I am not mistaken, we parted ways. Daniel Atijas joined a group of hikers, I believe—among them was the woman who had peered over the cliff edge—and he went with them down to the foot of the mountain without noticing, or, perhaps, not wanting to notice, the small, secret signs hinting of my presence. I let them get ahead, then slowly, more slowly than I would ever walk on the prairie, I set out along the winding trail among the pines. When I neared the end, my hopes swelled that I might come across Daniel Atijas waiting for me at Saint Julian Road. From the start he had struck me as a person who makes good on his promises, even when he hasn't sworn to them before witnesses. There was, however, no one on the trail, and after a brief hesitation I went on toward the Centre. News always travels faster than people do, especially bad news, and none of the people I passed on my way passed me without commenting on the, in the words of the Toronto playwright, "pointless death," which only enraged me all the more, because I doubt that any death can be said to have a point. I hurried further along among the buildings and was on my way to the studio, believing I could find a solitary passage there into another world, which, I confess, is only another name for the bottle of cognac I kept on the kitchen shelf. In the area between the small practice huts for musicians, right where the path ran that led to the roomier studios for writers and painters, stood two elks. They were still, their necks gently bowed, and they seemed to be listening to the strains of a cello, which, low and muted, reached them from one of the huts. I waved at them, thinking it might unnerve them and persuade them to back away, but they paid me not the slightest heed. To circumvent them I had to climb partway up a hill and then come down through the woods, and suddenly, as I pushed apart the bushes through which I was clambering, I felt a crushing exhaustion, so much so that I barely resisted lying down right there on the ground strewn with pine needles and leaves. If I had, I know I never would have gotten up again. I stepped over a fallen tree and returned to the path. There was only a short walk from there to my studio, but I had the impression that I would never get there or would fall asleep midstride and keep walking while asleep to the ends of the earth. At one point it seemed as if someone was walking behind me, but when I turned, I saw no one, elk or human. The next minute someone seemed to be walking ahead of me, or lurking behind a bush by the path, but when I neared the spot, there was no one there, though there was a scrap of red cloth, flamelike, on a twig. I don't know what time it was when I finally stepped into the studio, but by the time I left it, night had fallen. I drank some cognac, of that I'm certain, just as I am certain that I found no passage to another world. While I was drinking I studied the drawings again, sequencing them toward the greatest openness, making minor changes in only one or, perhaps, two places, adjusting the sequence. I picked up the phone several times, but each time, after a slight, or longer, hesitation, I set the receiver back in the cradle. I sensed that Daniel Atijas was not in his room, and even if he had been there, I thought, he probably wouldn't have picked up the phone, but still, when I entered Lloyd Hall, I went first to his room and leaned an ear toward the door. No matter how hard I tried, however, I couldn't hear a thing, and all I smelled was my own foul breath. When I returned to my room, I saw that a folded sheet of paper had been pushed under the door. I unfolded it and examined both sides, but there was nothing written on it. First I don't hear, I thought, then I don't see: is it time to check if I am even alive? Then I recalled stories and movies about messages in invisible ink and embarked on bold experiments with water, soap, shaving lotion, graphite powder, and other substances. None of these gave results, which, I thought, probably was the intention of the person who had slipped the sheet of paper between the foot of the door and the rug. If this was a warning, I thought, then it warned of a void; if it was advice, it was also warning of a void, but between the two voids the difference was vast. The first void spoke of absence, of the absence of absence, while the second spoke of presence, of absence as fullness. I was convinced that this was the meaning of the blank sheet of paper, just as I was convinced that Daniel Atijas had slipped it into my room, and then, driven by that unconvincing thought, I dropped onto the bed and straightaway, fully clothed, fell fast asleep. I am more inclined, however, to believe that I wasn't sleeping, because what I saw when I dreamed might be better termed a vision, events observed with eyes wide open. There is always a moment in a dream or immediately after waking when a dreamer's consciousness alerts him to the fact that what he was seeing was a dream. A vision is more real than a dream, and instead of playing with events from the past, a vision is nearly all focused on the future. A dream is guesswork, and a vision is a warning, which means that they are in no way similar. What I saw, flung as I was across the bed like a bedspread, was about the future, no doubt about it. When the vision ceased, I was overcome by an exhaustion one never feels after regular sleep and by a longing to tell Daniel Atijas about all of this, even though he was leaving soon, but I knew that after everything that had happened, I had to wait for morning, just as I knew that I should show him the portraits in the sequence in which I had laid them out in the studio, no matter what. This didn't mean that I saw any connection between the drawings and the vision, but if there was something they had in common, it was how they were different. The portraits spoke of calm and superiority, while the vision expressed agitation and debacle, the only similarity being that I perceived the vision as a sequence of scenes, just as the portrait was a sequence of drawings. The vision, in brief, showed my country in flames. I was surprised, frozen, and resisted with every ounce of my being, because everything in me said something like that could not happen. Canada in flames! When Daniel Atijas mentioned the possibility, I had dismissed it flatly, but now I saw, clear as a bell, how buildings in Montreal were toppling, how Indians battled the Quebecois, or rather fought a detachment of Quebec police who appeared from somewhere, apparently having trained for years, and I saw the fresh scalps of white men and Indians hanging from the branches of century-old trees, and then clashes broke out within the Quebec police, Quebecois against Anglo-Quebecers, and then volunteers from Ontario and Manitoba joined the fray; at the same time, in the left corner of my field of vision, Indians from British Columbia declared their reservations to be free territory, white racists from Alberta shot the first Arabs and Chinese, the prairie was ablaze in Saskatchewan, and only in the Atlantic provinces was there a deceptive calm, though the first skirmishes had begun on the streets of Halifax and in the rural areas of Newfoundland. The sky was glowing red over the North Pole, the polar ice cap was melting, and no one knew what to do, especially when the tower on the parliament building in Ottawa swayed slowly, then faster and faster, until it fell. Then I awoke, or maybe it's that I fell asleep, or lay there confused in the dark as it grew lighter. Who can say? Perhaps all of it happened at once, perhaps it is happening still, perhaps the past comprises all possibilities, and we, at an easy arm's length, choose the options that suit us best? I hadn't had a chance to talk about this with Daniel Atijas, though I meant to tell him about the dream, to hear what he'd have to say, and to put forward the ideas prompted by the vision, if it was a vision. When I finally wrenched free of the labyrinth of visual impressions just as the room was growing visible, I realized I should paint this vision of mine as a triptych of vast dimensions, with many allusions to William Blake and Hieronymus Bosch. I also resolved to read Dante again, though I am not sure why. In that, I thought, Daniel Atijas was the person who could have helped, but the day, the last day he spent at the Art Centre, was too short, he told me when I called him, for all the things other people had planned for his departure. He was to have lunch with the director of the Literary Arts Programs and the director's wife, dinner with the president of the Art Centre and his wife, and he hoped to make the rounds of the places he liked, do his last shopping, return books to the library, and then, around ten in the evening, he was going to get together with Mark Robinson and the other artists he had become close to one way or another and have a farewell drink. It wouldn't be bad, Daniel Atijas remarked, for me to join them, which I refused with disgust, of course, though I tried to keep the disgust from showing, claiming that I was tired and upset. Then breakfast is all we have left, said Daniel Atijas, because shortly after breakfast, as he had been informed by the office of the director of the Literary Arts Programs, someone would be shuttling him to the Calgary airport. Would he be able, before he went to breakfast, to stop by my studio? I asked, explaining that I had something to show him. He was not keen, I could hear that in his voice, but he agreed. He was planning for breakfast at eight, he said, and he could stop by my studio fifteen minutes beforehand if that suited me. Suits me, I said, and hung up. Maybe I was wrong not to accept his invitation to attend the send-off with the artists from the Art Centre, but I didn't regret it. I'd see Mark Robinson after Daniel Atijas left whether I wanted to or not, and the others I didn't care about anyway; they, at any rate, cared nothing for me. And after all, I knew they'd be getting together at the little restaurant in the Sally Borden building, and I could have gone over to join them had I wanted to. I got myself ready, therefore, for a very long day, figuring it would be best to spend it completely dedicated to making sense of my vision. I also decided I would eat nothing that day, which seemed appropriate for one intending to devote oneself entirely to the spirit. The cleansing of the body can only contribute to the elevation of ideas, no doubt about it. I intended to drink just water and, when I went to bed, mint tea. During the afternoon, using the side stairs and moving from one tree to the next, I left Lloyd Hall and went to my studio. The day was sunny and warm, and a man and a woman only in bathing suits were playing tennis. A squirrel was sitting on a chain-link fence. When I was near the practice huts for musicians and thought I was finally safe, Guy Fletcher stepped out in front of me. He turned up like a ghost, though ghosts do not usually turn up in broad daylight, and it transpired that, like all ghosts, he was bearing news from the other side. When he had heard yesterday, said Guy Fletcher, of the tragedy on Tunnel Mountain, he was almost sick, because only the day before in the early afternoon, Ivan Matulić's grandson had stopped by to see him at the museum and had left something there for Daniel Atijas. He extended to me a small package wrapped in white paper and secured with crisscrossed rubber bands. He had tried to find Daniel Atijas in his room, he said, but Daniel Atijas wasn't there, so he thought he'd come over to my studio, figuring it would be best to give me the package, but there was no one there either, he said and it was a lucky thing, he said, that we'd met, because he was beginning to despair, convinced that he would not be able to fulfill the last wishes, he could say that now, of the deceased. I stared at the white package in his hands as if it hid some sort of time bomb. I reached out slowly and touched it with my fingertips; then I took it and drew it in to myself. It was light, much lighter than I'd expected, and Daniel Atijas's name had been written on it in the right lower corner in uneven letters with a thick felt-tip pen. He was almost sick, Guy Fletcher told me, because of the words that Ivan Matulić's grandson had said at the time, and which only later, when he learned of the accident, revealed themselves in their true meaning. The grandson, Guy Fletcher continued, had said he was leaving things he knew he would not be needing anymore, since he no longer needed anything. Sometimes, the grandson told him, it is great to be stripped bare. And only when the bad news reached him, said Guy Fletcher, did he grasp the meaning of these words, the meaning of the nakedness. He looked me straight in the eyes. I didn't know what he saw in them, but in his I saw tears. I patted him on the shoulder and told him not to worry, that the package had come to the right hands and that I would definitely pass it on to Daniel Atijas as soon as the opportunity arose. Guy Fletcher thanked me, and having said that he still had to get back to the museum, he hurried downhill toward the parking lot. I waited for him to get beyond the administrative building, and then, right there on the little bridge, I pulled away the rubber bands and tore the paper. The edge of a soft cardboard box appeared. I opened that as well, actually ripped it open, and out of the gaping tear there began to fall photographs, postcards, sheets of paper with writing on them, notes with little drawings and smudged scrawls. Then an envelope appeared, small, all white, on which in the same uneven letters was the name Daniel Atijas. If there was something that resembled a human heart, I thought, then this envelope was it. I leaned over and began collecting the scattered bits of paper and photographs, and only then, when my head was near the ground, did I hear the muted sound of a flute, though it could have been the sound of a clarinet or a recorder, because except for the piccolo and the saxophone, all wind instruments sounded the same to me. I quickly had all the papers in my hands, and hugging them to my chest, I walked, slightly bent over, over to the studio. No one saw me, I met no one, but just in case, I locked the door and drew the curtains. I looked over the photographs, leafed through the sheets of paper with writing and the notes, picked out the blades of grass and twigs I had inadvertently gathered up with them. I leaned the little envelope on a glass that was standing in the middle of the table. Everything that was in the package, in the torn box, all the photographs and pages covered in text, had to do with Ivan Matulić's grandson's time spent in Croatia. I assumed that the pages came from his diary, or perhaps this was his whole diary, supplemented with postcards and photographs, some of which, judging by who was in them, he had taken himself, whereas others had been taken by someone else. I did not make an effort to read anything, just as I did not open the white envelope. Though I didn't know what was written in the letter inside it, I could make an educated guess: all he had discovered on his travels, on his journey into the heart of darkness, Ivan Matulić's grandson was leaving to Daniel Atijas, convinced that he, Daniel Atijas, was on a journey headed in the opposite direction, away from the darkness and into the light, and there is nothing that so inspires us to embrace the goodness of the light as a constant reminder of the ominous nature of darkness. There are those who leave others the legacy of a torch, a beacon that shines, while someone else endows an absence of radiance, a black hole, a monster under the bed. I inferred all this from the letter in the white envelope, and then my head drooped, and I rested my forehead on the table surface. I knew, without trying to explain the reasons to myself, that I would not give Daniel Atijas the letter, but I did not know what to do with it. I could, for instance, have gone to the Banff cemetery and buried it there by a tombstone, along with the rest of the papers and photographs. I also could have tossed it into the river and made paper boats out of the sheets of paper with writing and set them sailing after it. I could have gone into the woods, found a hollow tree, and thrown all the papers into it, including the unopened letter. A squirrel, I thought, would have been glad for such a cozy nest. Then I got up, went into the kitchen, found matches, and slowly, over the sink, burned everything: the photographs, the sheets of paper with writing and the notes, and finally the little white envelope. The paper burned quickly, easily; flames of different colors flickered up from the photographs; the envelope twisted, puffed, and stretched, then suddenly burned all at once, as if the fire were eating it from the inside. I turned on the faucet and rinsed the sooty remains down the sink and off my fingers. I remembered the box and the paper that everything was wrapped in, so I burned that, too, piece by piece. The only things I didn't burn were the rubber bands, which I left in the drawer with the eating utensils, though just in case I wiped them off well with a towel, first a damp one, then a dry one. I opened the window, carefully inspected the sink and the whole kitchen, and then sat again at the table. I was satisfied. I could breathe more easily: aside from the smell of smoke that was still on my fingers, which wouldn't last long, there was nothing that said there had ever been a package from Ivan Matulić's grandson. My head drooped again, and, a little faster this time, I rested my forehead on the table. I will not fall asleep, I remember thinking, and then I woke up in pitch-black darkness, in the middle of the night, with a crick in my neck and dry lips. At first I was convinced that I had found myself in a sea of absolute silence, but then, gradually, I was able to discern the nocturnal sounds, the crunching, scratching, panting, humming, so in the end I had to wonder how I had ever been able to fall asleep, and after that, of course, even when I lay down on the narrow cot, against the rules that forbade sleeping in the studios, sleep did not come easily. At exactly seven forty-five Daniel Atijas knocked at my door. He was in a white shirt, jeans, and sneakers, freshly shaven, neatly combed, ready to travel. I invited him in, and he reminded me as he entered that he had only fifteen minutes because at exactly eight he had to be at breakfast. He did not say who he'd be seeing there, but to be frank, that had ceased to interest me. I was tired, underslept, nervous, and I wanted to get it over with as soon as possible, to see him leave, travel away, and show up finally in that unfortunate country of his. Before this it had already occurred to me that my vision had been the result of his visit, and that he should be held in quarantine, stripped of his right to move about freely—not only he but everyone from there—until the world was sure they had stopped spreading the contagion of conflict and destruction. Several days ago, I know, such a thought would never have crossed my mind, but now everything was different, including me. We could waste no time, however, since both he and I were in a hurry, and fifteen minutes is not much, so I stepped back from the door, let him in, offered him a seat, put a cup of coffee in front of him, along with a sugar bowl and a dish with honey, and then, almost in the same movement, without losing a moment, I continued to the other side of the studio, where I brought the pad with the pile of draw-ings from. Until then I had thought it would be enough just to set it down on the table and have him look through the drawings, but as I came over clutching the pad tightly, our eyes met, and I saw that he was expecting me to say something. He hadn't struck me as the type of person to whom one needed to explain one's actions, but that was when we'd first met, and now, after every-thing that had happened, there was nothing I could be certain of. I looked at my watch: thirteen more minutes until eight. I told him I would like his opinion on the drawings I was putting in front of him, drawings I had spent many hours on over the past weeks, so in a multitude of different ways, which I would not go into now, I said, they were connected to his presence in Banff, and I felt it was important to show them to him despite the pres-sure he was certainly under as he prepared to go, for during these last days, I said, I had come to value the aptness and subtlety of his ability to gauge things, and an appraisal such as his, as he must know from his own experience, could be decisive motivation for further work or, indeed, for giving up altogether, since it would allow the artist to jettison needless ballast. I had not meant to sound like such a sycophant, but sometimes words say what they want to say, and there is nothing we can do about it. I looked at my watch again: eleven minutes to go. I opened the pad with the drawings and sat across from him. On the first drawing, a gently curving line depicting a furrowed brow, he spent almost a minute. Then he leafed through the drawings faster and faster, halting at those that drew his attention—for instance, one I had called

Thirteen Views of the Left Ear—though a little later, when the drawings became more complete and the figure on them more visible, he slowed the rhythm of his leafing, and perhaps just when he had come to the drawing on which all the individual elements first formed a whole, at that moment, he seemed to stop breathing altogether. It was five to eight, and a minute later, at four to eight, he glanced at his watch and said that soon he would have to be going. The face was still disintegrating within the space of the drawing, sometimes it even slipped off and then reappeared, full of empty spaces, but in the next two or three minutes it became quite clearly defined, though this was maybe only my impression, since I was sitting across from Daniel Atijas, and the whole time, despite the angle at which I was looking at his real face, I could compare the elements of the drawings with details of the model. At precisely eight o'clock, Daniel Atijas raised the last drawing, studied it while holding it to the light, as if looking for the watermark in the sheet of paper, and then turned it and laid it on the pile with the others. He looked at me over the table, and for a moment I thought he might reach over and put his hand on mine. He did not, of course, do that. He is waiting, I thought, for me to say something first, but I really did not know what to say. I looked at the clock and saw the big hand shiver and move a notch. As if he had been waiting for this, Daniel Atijas got up, lifted the drawings, and flipped over the bundle so that the wavy furrow was on top. He touched it, cautiously, as if it were piping hot, and then he turned, mumbled that he was late, and headed for the door. I didn't have to look at the clock again. I got up from the chair and hurried after him. He was already on the path, among the shadows, and here, once he had moved away a little, he stopped and raised his arm. I raised mine, my right arm, and so we stood, without a word, without a breath, in the morning freshness, and though I knew his departure was inevitable, at that moment he looked like someone who had nowhere to go. And then he left. He began walking faster and faster until he broke into a run and disappeared at the bottom of the path. For a moment I had the thought that I should go after him, that I should go to the dining hall for breakfast or at least find a private spot where I could watch him leave, but I went back to the studio, shut the door, and went over to the table. I sat in the chair on which he had just been sitting: it was still warm. I reached over and touched the furrow on the paper exactly where he had touched it. I suddenly thought that I'd be back on the plains again soon, and I was glad.

AFTERWORD
Only Banff Is Real

In the opening pages of *Globetrotter*, the painter (never named) from Saskatchewan searches for the right way to strike up a conversation with the Serbian Jewish writer Daniel Atijas. The two men are fellows at the art center nestled in the Banff National Park in the heart of the Canadian Rockies. After exploring several avenues, and still determined to start a conversation, the protagonist settles on the strategy of musing out loud about what kind of a novel he, a painter, might write about Banff.

Like his character Daniel Atijas, David Albahari was a writing fellow at the Banff Centre when he first came to Canada from Serbia in the middle of the wars of the 1990s. I had been translating Albahari's stories since we first met in the late 1980s, while both of us were still living in what was then Yugoslavia: he in Belgrade, I in Zagreb. I returned to my native Boston in 1990, and Albahari came to Canada to be a resident in Banff in 1994. The first I heard of the Banff Centre was when Albahari faxed me an essay during his residency so that he could read it, in my translation, to a gathering of the fellows. I recently found fragments of it in the depths of my computer and was able to salvage this passage:

> On the first floor and part of the second was the local book-store. When I discovered it on my second day in Banff, I closely perused the shelves with books of prose and poetry and, by habit, pulled out the books I wanted to own. Then, one by one, I put them back on the shelves where I'd found them. The rest of the books had already begun to expand, taking over the newly emptied spaces, but I was persistent. I repeated this ritual, which I have developed over the past two or three years, denying myself any opportunity of bringing a book home with me from a trip. It took the war for me to understand the futility of all property; despite my intention to "wander free as a bird," I had accumulated belongings, I had hoarded, I had stuck to things like a caterpillar sticks to a leaf, but when I greeted Jewish refugees from Sarajevo, each one spoke of "his" books, of despair at the thought that "someone else's foot" was kicking them around or "someone else's hands" were tossing them into flames.

We never learn what the painter or Daniel Atijas might have written about his stay in Banff, but *Globetrotter* is the Banff novel that David Albahari wrote; it was originally published in Serbian in 2001 and has been translated into French and now English.

The novels that Albahari wrote during his eighteen years in Canada create together a sort of meta-narrative. Each one functions well on its own, and each is quite distinct from all the others, yet if you read two, or three, or all of them, you will enjoy a rich interplay of images and perspectives, absences and presences.

The short stories he was writing before he moved to Canada secured his standing within Serbian literature and inaugurated themes he has explored ever since; a selection are published in English translation in *Words Are Something Else*. He has also shone as a translator of such American writers as John Barth, Robert Coover, and Thomas Pynchon. Like the works he has chosen to translate, his short stories have been postmodern and experimental. Throughout his writing career he has employed a dark, feverish humor, and Albahari, it is fair to say, is obsessed by obsession. All of his prose is structured around bickering, dueling voices; he uses those voices to poke at the nature of fiction, art, history, to illuminate his characters, to move his story forward. A thread that runs through his work is the nature of presence and absence, which is particularly pertinent to his Canadian novels, since his absence from Serbia has so clearly defined the presence, in Serbia, of his writing.

Except for *Götz and Meyer*, Albahari's Canadian novels, *Bait, Snow Man, Leeches, Globetrotter*, and *Darkness* (*Mrak*; the only one that has not yet been translated into English), have many common threads. Each features a writer. Jewish characters appear in almost all of them. Native Americans and their lore have their place, as does talk about the nature of words and writing. And the war is always an absent presence, dictating the narrative from a distance. It is only with *Leeches* that Albahari brings his story home to the hostilities shaping Serbian life in the late 1990s, although even *Leeches* is narrated from abroad, possibly Canada, to which the narrator is forced to flee. *Götz and Meyer* is the one exception among the Canadian novels, for the story explores the fate of Jews in Serbia during World War II; it begins and ends in Belgrade.

Unlike the writer-protagonists of *Snow Man* and *Leeches*, the protagonist of *Globetrotter* is a painter; the writer is the novel's object rather than its subject. The counterpoint of conversation between the protagonist painter and the writer Daniel Atijas allows for a lively discussion about art that uses paint, and art that uses words. Atijas comes up with the engaging notion that the best stories "start from the middle and then, a little like a tangled skein, resist anyone's predictions about how they will unravel." The bickering voices of the two men are joined by a third interlocutor—Ivan Matulić's grandson—and the complexity of the competing narratives feeds the novel's thriller-like tension.

In June of 2011, I arrived in Banff. My project at a three-week translation residency was to translate Albahari's *Globetrotter* into English. The Banff International Literary Translation Centre invited the author to attend as well, so David Albahari joined us there for five days. Although he and I have been working together for twenty-five years, we have been in the same room only a few times.

Together we went to the Museum of Natural History and

looked at the stuffed owls, the lynx, the grizzly. Together we went into town from the Centre, walking by the cemetery, and roamed the streets, which really do have animal names like Badger, Otter, Wolf, Bear, Buffalo, Grizzly, Rabbit. We went to the Banff Springs Hotel and had coffee on the terrace near where the Spray flows into the Bow, on a bluff overlooking the two rivers and the Fairholme Range with its snow-covered peaks.

While Albahari was in Banff with us translators in 2011, he wrote a piece about our residency, which I translated on the spot and he and I read at one of our gatherings. It is entitled "The Banff Translators."

Once they had finished translating everything there was to translate in Banff, the Banff translators, better known as Group 25, headed east. Along the way they translated all they saw: they translated elks into buffalo, Japanese tourists into an Aboriginal of the Blackfoot Tribe, the mayor of Calgary into Chief Sitting Bull. The squirrels in all languages remained the same, as did the words: cage, peanut, love, and communism. By then the translators had reached the East Coast of North America and here for the first time they were faced in all seriousness by their role in the world and life. It had been a breeze to be a translator in Banff, but how, now, to translate fish into gulls, salt into iodine, German submarines into optical cables, and the flushed cheeks of newly grown girls into the first dreams that would flush their faces even more? There was no help to be had here from the Old English, the Sanskrit, and the Celtic languages. Love is untranslatable, unless replaced by pure energy, such as: waves lapping at the toes of the Banff translators. The translators are barefoot as they have learned meanwhile that for a translation to be good there has to be first-hand, or first-foot, experience, their feet must feel the mud of the earth first if they are to catch sight later of the gleam of stars, there is an order which defies translation, and untranslatable is a breath or a heartbeat or that soft sound when tooth hits tooth at the end of a first kiss.

Back home in Calgary, Albahari was packing his bags to move back to Serbia. A few months later, in 2012, he made the move. These two stays in Banff, his as a writer in 1994 and mine as his translator in 2011, are, in a sense, bookends for his eighteen Canadian years.

Albahari has continued writing. Since his return to Serbia he has published four novels, which herald a new poetic and new, sharply provocative themes. In the spirit of this novel's attention to presence and absence, it is worth saying that the translation of his novels into English guarantees him an English-language presence regardless of where he chooses to absent or present himself.

Novels and stories by David Albahari available in English:

Words Are Something Else, translated by Ellen Elias-Bursać

Tsing, translated by David Albahari

Bait, translated by Peter Agnone

Snow Man, translated by Ellen Elias-Bursać

Götz and Meyer, translated by Ellen Elias-Bursać

Leeches, translated by Ellen Elias-Bursać

Learning Cyrillic, translated by Ellen Elias-Bursać

ELLEN ELIAS-BURSAĆ

DAVID ALBAHARI (b. 1948), a Serbian writer and translator, has published eleven collections of short stories and thirteen novels, all in Serbian, including *Shadows* (short stories, 2006) and *Leeches* (novel, 2005). His *Description of Death* won the Ivo Andrić Award for the best book of short stories published in Yugoslavia in 1982. *Bait* won the NIN Prize for the best novel published in Yugoslavia in 1996, as well as the Balcanica Award and the Berlin Bridge Prize. His books have been translated into sixteen languages. Two collections of short stories and six novels have been published in English.

David Albahari has translated into Serbian many books by contemporary British, American, Australian, and Canadian authors, including stories and novels by Saul Bellow, Isaac Bashevis Singer, Thomas Pynchon, Margaret Atwood, V. S. Naipaul, and Vladimir Nabokov. He has also translated plays by Sam Shepard, Sarah Kane, Caryl Churchill, and Jason Sherman.

He is a member of the Serbian Academy of Science and Arts.

In 1994 he moved to Calgary, Canada, with his wife and two children; since 2012 he has been spending more of his time in Serbia.

ELLEN ELIAS-BURSAĆ has been translating novels and nonfiction by Bosnian, Croatian, and Serbian writers for more than twenty years. She has translated two books of short stories and four novels by David Albahari, as well as works by Daša Drndić, Antun Šoljan, Dubravka Ugrešić, and Karim Zaimović.

Her translation of David Albahari's book of short stories *Words*

Are Something Else received the translation award of the American Association of Teachers of Slavic and East European Languages (AATSEEL) in 1998, and her translation of Albahari's novel *Götz and Meyer* received the National Translation Award of the American Literary Translation Association (ALTA) in 2006. She received a National Endowment for the Arts (NEA) translation fellowship and was a fellow at the Banff International Literary Translation Centre in 2011.